A TIME TO HEAL

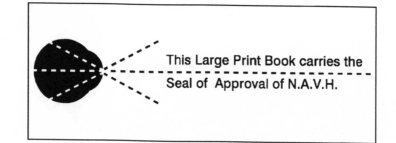

This Large Print Book carries the
Seal of Approval of N.A.V.H.

A TIME TO HEAL

LINDA GOODNIGHT

THORNDIKE PRESS
A part of Gale, Cengage Learning

Detroit • New York • San Francisco • New Haven, Conn • Waterville, Maine • London

Copyright © 2008 by Linda Goodnight.
Thorndike Press, a part of Gale, Cengage Learning.

ALL RIGHTS RESERVED

Thorndike Press® Large Print Christian Romance.
The text of this Large Print edition is unabridged.
Other aspects of the book may vary from the original edition.
Set in 16 pt. Plantin.
Printed on permanent paper.

LIBRARY OF CONGRESS CATALOGING-IN-PUBLICATION DATA

Goodnight, Linda.
    A time to heal / by Linda Goodnight.
      p. cm. — (Thorndike Press large print Christian romance)
    ISBN-13: 978-1-4104-1495-3 (alk. paper)
    ISBN-10: 1-4104-1495-7 (alk. paper)
    1. Women physicians—Fiction. 2. First loves—Fiction. 3.
Oklahoma—Fiction. 4. Large type books. I. Title.
PS3557.O5857T56 2009
813'.54—dc22
                                         2008056119

Published in 2009 by arrangement with Harlequin Books S.A.

Printed in the United States of America
1 2 3 4 5 6 7 13 12 11 10 09

"For I know the plans I have for you,"
declares the Lord.
"Plans to prosper you and not to harm
you, plans to give you hope and a future."

— *Jeremiah* 29:11

This one is for you, the faithful readers who buy my books, who write me letters and e-mails filled with sweet encouragement. I am grateful for every single one of you. You are a blessing.

CHAPTER ONE

"I'm never going back."

Dr. Kathryn Thatcher lay in the wooden porch swing, one arm slung across her eyes, her weary body soaking up sun.

She hadn't been outside in such a long time she'd likely suffer second-degree burn. But the old family home at Wilson's Cove, Oklahoma, was tailor-made for lazing around, something the career-driven Dr. Thatcher never did. Until now.

Three days and counting since she'd asked her medical director for a leave of absence and walked out. In truth, she wanted to resign, but he'd talked her out of it. Didn't matter. She was done, finished, through.

Too many dead kids would do that to a person.

"A few days' rest and you'll be ready to go again. You're just tired."

Kat's sister, Susan Renfro, sat on the top step of the long wooden porch, fingers laced around one knee, short dark unruly curls gleaming in the sunlight. She'd gained more weight, something Kat was not about to mention, considering Susan had never lost the extra twenty pounds from Sadie's birth four years ago. Three kids and a love for Southern comfort cooking had destroyed her sister's former cheerleader body.

Who was she to talk? She'd added a few pounds, too, and her idea of exercise was running from one exam room to another.

"I'm more than tired, Suz," Kat said, though she couldn't deny the exhaustion. "Maybe I made a mistake. Maybe I wasn't cut out for the medical profession."

Memories of that last, terrible night pressed in. Kat shivered, still hearing the incessant rain hammering against the glass E.R. doors as ambulance after ambulance arrived, carrying victims from a five-car pileup on I-35. Thirty-six hours of blood and death, the worst of it being that all the fatalities were teenagers.

"A career in medicine is all you ever wanted, Kat. It's who you are."

Lately, Kat wasn't sure who she was or what she wanted.

Her older sister meant well, but she had no idea what an E.R. physician's life was like.

Like most girls in Wilson's Cove, Susan married her high school sweetheart the summer after graduation and settled down around the 700-acre recreational lake, content to raise a family and take care of the family's rental cabins. She'd never gone to college, much less spent years working eighty hours a week until she was a zombie inside and out. She'd also never had to bear the news to parents that their beautiful, fresh-faced sixteen-year-old would never graduate from high school.

"Becoming a doctor was all I wanted as a kid. I'm not a kid anymore." She'd gone into medicine to save lives. Lately, all she'd done was sign death certificates.

"Then, what do you want?"

"I don't know." There was the truth. She wanted to be happy. She wanted to feel joy. She wanted some intangible something that lacked definition. But if she admitted as much, she'd get a sermon. To her sister, life revolved around faith in God. That was fine for Susan. Religion hadn't worked so well for Kathryn. She and God had let each other down a long time ago.

"I'm being sued," she said.

"For what?" Susan frowned and sat up straighter, ready to defend her baby sister. The sight warmed a cold spot inside of

Kathryn. That was the great thing about family and one of the things she'd forgotten in her long absences from the cove.

"For being a doctor, I guess. I never even saw the patient, but I wrote and signed a discharge summary for his chart. Therefore, I am as liable for his death as the blood clot that killed him."

"That's ridiculous."

"Happens all the time." Another reason she was back in Wilson's Cove for good. She was tired of fighting the system.

"What are you going to do about it?"

"Nothing I can do except let the lawyers duke it out." And sit by while her malpractice insurance jumped into yet another exorbitant bracket.

"Well, that's just wrong."

Kat agreed, resentment boiling up inside her like a geyser. But if she followed that train of thought, she'd have a stroke.

Closing her eyes, she tried not to think at all, a major problem for a woman whose mind never stopped churning. She was always thinking, always working, always planning. Sometimes she wanted to scream for her mind to shut up.

April was here and, oh, how she loved the wild Oklahoma spring. With iron determination, she concentrated on the sights and sounds, anything to wash away the memories of her work in Oklahoma City.

Lilacs and peach blossoms scented the air with gentle sweetness, and the hum of bees and other insects filled the afternoon. A butterfly hovered on one of Susan's geranium pots, a splash of yellow on fuchsia. Spring meant new beginnings, new growth, the rebirth of nature after a long, hard winter. For a silly moment, Kat wished she could be a tulip or a daffodil, ready to burst into newness.

"Guess who I saw this morning?" Susan asked after a long period of silence.

"I give up," Kat said, lazily opened her eyes to peer into Susan's clear blue ones. "Who?"

With a Cheshire Cat grin, Susan tugged at the toe of Kat's tennis shoe. "Seth Washington. He asked about you."

Kathryn's stomach quivered, and she sat up, pulling her foot away. Even though Susan had made a point of keeping her apprised of Seth's life ever since he moved back to Wilson's Cove last year, Kat tried never to think about the boy she'd loved in high school.

"How did he know I was here?"

"Oh, come on, Kat. This is Wilson's Cove. Everyone in town knew you were home fifteen minutes after you stopped for gas at the Quick Mart."

"Oh." She'd almost forgotten the invisible information line that zinged from one side of the lake to the other, especially when the news concerned one of its own. The summer people came, camped, fished and left. But Kat's family had been here long before Wilson's Lake became a popular vacation spot, had owned most of the land at one time. The locals knew her, were proud of her, too, because she'd gone off to the big city to become a doctor.

Well, now she was back. Wonder what they'd think of that?

"Aren't you curious about him?" Susan was relentless when she got something into her head. And Seth Washington seemed to be her favorite subject whenever she talked to her baby sister.

"No." They'd had this conversation before.

Kat finished off an icy glass of Susan's fresh lemonade to prove how uninterested she was. In the few times she'd been back to the cove, she'd made a pointed effort to avoid the new lake ranger. "Not interested."

"Liar." Her sister swatted Kat's lily-white leg. "I'm going to tell you anyway. Donna down at the Quick Mart says he's divorced. Has been for a long time, though he kept

14

dinner while I put together the chicken casserole."

Kat groaned for effect before setting to work. Actually, she didn't mind helping in the kitchen as long as Susan didn't ask her to fry chicken or make gravy. Her idea of a home-cooked meal was microwavable Lean Cuisine. The rest of the time she lived on machine sandwiches, and doughnuts left in the doctor's lounge by drug reps looking to make brownie points.

Other than knowing medicine, Dr. Thatcher was pretty much useless, a grim reality considering her decision to leave the field behind.

Susan, on the other hand, was Miss Susie Homemaker in the flesh. She loved to cook, sew and constantly tried out new ideas for renovating the old farmhouse or the rental cabins. Last year she'd gone into Colonial mode and painted all the cabinets blue. Currently, she was trying her hand at faux finishes. The woman never stopped creating and beautifying the world. It was who she was, a fact that kept Kat from complaining about Susan's attempts to "fix up" her life in the same way she fixed up houses.

Kathryn took a fat potato from the bowl, challenging herself to peel the spud in one long curly piece.

"I'm moving over to the cabin tomorrow," she said.

"Did you ask Danny?" Susan's husband was in real estate and handled most of the rental property around the lake.

"It's my house." She lifted a shoulder to scratch her itchy nose. "Why would I have to ask Danny?"

"Because you told him to rent it out. You're never here."

"I'm here now." Kat caught her bottom lip under her top teeth and stilled the flow of irritation. She *had* told Danny to rent the place. No use getting huffy now. "Is my cabin rented out?"

"Yes, it is." Slowly wrapping an onion in plastic wrap, Susan turned to look at her. "Is staying with us so bad?"

"You have three kids, Suz. This place is Grand Central Station."

"But the house is big and roomy. And you could use some TLC from the people who love you and can put up with your arrogant moods."

"I am neither arrogant nor moody."

"Ho-ho! And wet dogs don't stink. This is your big sister you're talking to. I know all your secrets."

The thought grabbed Kat right in the center of her chest and squeezed. No, Susan didn't know one of her secrets. But Seth Washington did.

Kat loved her sister and the noisy bunch of nieces and nephew, but she also needed her own space. After dinner she made excuses and went for a walk to clear her head.

The family home rested more than two hundred yards back from Wilson's Lake, but the water sounds and smells carried on the breeze. A familiar trail led through the trees and underbrush to the shoreline. Still another meandered to the east toward Kat's cabin. Without conscious decision, she headed in that direction, curious to see who resided there in her absence. After all the effort she'd put into making the cabin a lovely retreat, Kat didn't want to live anywhere else. Maybe she could convince the renter to find another place now that she was home.

As she traversed the woods, a thousand other thoughts plagued her. She worried about the effect her abrupt departure from the medical center would have on the other staff members, about the patients she'd turned over to other physicians, but most of all she wondered about the future. As clichéed as it sounded, today was the first day of the rest of her life, and she didn't know

21

what to do with it. She'd worked too long and too hard to remain idle for any extended period of time.

The old trail hadn't been used in a while and the blackberry thickets were taking over. Thorny vines, sprinkled with tiny white flowers, reached out and grabbed her exposed legs. She slowed long enough to direct the growth elsewhere, mentally marking the spot for later in the summer when black, juicy berries could become a cobbler. In Susan's capable hands, of course. Certainly not hers.

As she rounded into the clearing at the side of Kat's Cabin, as the family had dubbed the two-bedroom cottage, her spirits lifted. Though she spent little time here, she felt better knowing the small A-frame was available when she needed a break. And boy, did she need the familiar comfort of home right now.

The air was alive with spring smells and sounds, but her house was quiet. A bright-red riding mower was parked beneath a drooping mimosa tree in the front yard. Someone had recently cut the grass, but that someone was nowhere to be seen.

Kat craned her head toward the backyard where the fishing dock extended far into the lake. No one there, either.

She knocked and the action felt odd given this was her house. When no one answered, she reached under the top porch step. When her fingers touched the plastic holder, she grinned. The key was right where she'd left it.

Telling herself that she only wanted to check the place out, to make sure the renter was taking care of her property, Kat opened the door and stepped inside.

Nothing much had changed. Her living room furniture, a comfortable mix of favorite pieces, had been moved around to accommodate a big-screen TV. A basket of folded laundry rested on the couch and several magazines were stacked neatly on her maple end table.

Out of curiosity she moved closer, saw the laundry was mostly men's shirts and socks, and the top magazine was a recent edition of *True Crime.* So, a guy had rented her cabin. At least he was fairly neat.

She wandered into the kitchen, found the room tidy and clean except for a peanut butter jar on the counter and a butter knife and a glass in the sink. Though she'd had no qualms about entering the cabin, she opted against climbing the steps to the loft bedrooms. A bedroom was personal and private.

Crossing to the rounded row of windows that looked from the country kitchen toward the lake, she peered out. The lake was serene; the fading sun glowed orange and gold across the glassy surface. In the distance a pair of boat fishermen stood silhouetted against the sky, fishing rods arched into the shimmering water. Kat breathed in slowly, deeply, refreshed just to be here. There was something so serene and calming about Wilson's Lake.

Susan was right. Kathryn needed time to rest and unwind. And there was no place better on earth than her own private, isolated cabin. Whoever lived here would simply have to move. Maybe she could make him a deal. She was willing to help him find a better place and pay the difference in rents. Her mental and emotional health was worth the expense. Money wasn't a problem. She had plenty of that. As a kid, she'd dreamed of the day she could say those words. But now that she had money, she never had time.

Well, she was taking the time.

Suddenly her tranquility was shattered. The front door banged opened, slammed against the wall and reverberated on its hinges.

Kat's heart behaved in much the same

way. It slammed hard against her rib cage.

A powerful voice yelled, "Put your hands in the air! Do it now!"

Kat spun around to explain, but the words froze on her lips. The biggest gun she'd ever seen pointed straight at her. Her mouth went dry and her knees began to tremble. She slowly raised both hands.

"Don't shoot," she squeaked, afraid to move, afraid to take her eyes off that deadly weapon. Had Danny rented her cottage to a serial killer? She started babbling. "I'm sorry. I should have waited for you to get home. I just . . ."

"Kat?" That quick, the man lowered the gun and stepped from the shadowed living room into the kitchen sunlight.

Kat's wobbly knees almost gave way.

Standing before her, looking fierce and manly and more ruggedly handsome than she remembered was Seth Washington.

CHAPTER TWO

"What do you think you're doing?" Grim-faced, Seth slid the Glock into his back waistband. "I could have shot you."

He stood glaring at her, stance wide, shoulders tense as if he still might.

How did she respond to *that?*

Blood pounded in her ears, and the metallic taste of fear burned in the back of her throat. Over the years she'd treated any number of gunshot wounds, and she knew the damage a weapon of that caliber could do to the human body. But she'd never had one pointed in her direction. A shudder passed over her.

Seth must have noticed her distress. He stalked across the room, gripped her upper arm with incredibly strong fingers and led her to a chair. She slid gratefully onto the cane-bottom seat. Seth moved away, ran some water and came back with a glass.

"Drink this."

She obeyed, gulping down the fresh well water in a vain attempt to cool the fire of adrenaline pumping through her blood at Mach-2 force. Fingers trembling against the glass humiliated and annoyed her. She was a confident woman, unflappable in an emergency. At the moment she was a mess.

Seth crouched in front of her chair, bringing with him the woodsy scent of outdoors. Head cocked to one side, he raked her face with hawklike scrutiny. His strong jaw flexed a couple of times and his nostrils flared. She wasn't sure if he was furious or worried.

A few times over the years, she'd fantasized about seeing him again, but this was one scenario that hadn't occurred to her. Not even close.

"You okay?" His voice had matured into a gravelly baritone, the gravel probably the result of yelling at people to get down or get their hands in the air. "I'm sorry if I scared you."

If he'd scared her? Who was he kidding?

With a deep cleansing breath, she set the glass onto the tabletop and stiffened her spine. "If this is the way you say hello to old friends, I'd hate to be your enemy."

The slightest glint of amusement lit his grass-green eyes. "Who said we were friends?"

His dark hair was cut short, but the springy waves that had given him fits in high school were still apparent. Here and there she spotted a single strand of silver amidst the black. She'd always liked his thick, wavy hair though he'd considered it too girly. She wondered if he still did and then inwardly laughed at herself. From wide, powerful shoulders to five-o'clock shadow, there was nothing girly about this new and mature Seth.

Off balance at noticing him at all, Kathryn fired back, "Too bad you never came into the E.R. when I was on duty. I would have stapled your smart mouth shut."

He laughed then, a bark of sound that bounced off the tiny kitchen walls and straight into Kat's memory. Seth had grown up tough, but in spite of his troubled home life, he'd been full of fun and laughter. Now she realized the behavior had probably been a coping mechanism. She hoped his adult life had given him real reasons for joy.

"Still the same snooty girl," he said, which made her grin. She'd been focused, shy and studious, three qualities that some had mistaken for snobbery, including Seth at first.

He pushed to a stand, his six-foot frame

towering above her, though she was not petite by any means. "So, how've you been, Kat?"

She didn't want to tell him the truth. That the dreams she'd chased had turned to nightmares. "I was about to ask you the same thing."

He scrubbed a hand over his face, and Kat caught the scratchy sound of day-old beard. "I'm okay. I like the ranger job. The offer came at a time when I was ready for a change."

Though curious, she didn't ask if the move had anything to do with his broken marriage. Too many years and tears had flowed by to ask such personal questions. "So you moved back home. I never would have expected that."

He lifted a uniform-clad shoulder. "Seemed like a good idea after —" He hesitated, and then smooth as a swan on water, redirected the conversation. Regardless, Kat caught his drift. A divorce would have been doubly hard on a steadfast man like Seth.

"Is there a legitimate reason why you decided to break into my house today?" he asked. "Or can I assume the medical field doesn't pay as well as rumored and you've taken to a life of crime."

She raised both hands to shoulder height. "Am I being interrogated, Officer?"

One corner of Seth's mouth kicked up, and Kat gave up trying not to notice how attractive he still was. Maybe even more so now. Where he'd been all planes and angles as a teenager, today he was muscular, fit and sturdy with not an ounce of fat on him.

"No interrogation necessary. I caught you red-handed."

"Would you really have shot me?"

His dark eyes went flat and cold as all the frivolity left him. A shiver danced up Kat's spine. Criminals must tremble at the sound of his name.

"Probably not, but we *have* been experiencing some break-ins lately."

"Susan didn't mention that."

"I've tried to keep things low-key for the time being. They mostly break in, mess the place up, help themselves to the food and booze, if there is any. A couple of places lost some cash and prescription drugs."

"That explains your jumpiness."

"I wasn't jumpy. If I had been, we would be having this conversation in an ambulance."

"Ouch. You're scaring me."

"Someone needs to. Even if your brother-in-law handles most of the property on the lake, you shouldn't be going into someone else's house when they aren't there."

"I admit that was pretty stupid. But actually, this is my house and I came over to talk you out of it."

"This is your cabin?" When she nodded, he pulled a chair around and straddled it, facing her. "Danny didn't tell me."

Danny knew the history between Kat and Seth. Maybe he'd thought to let sleeping dogs lie. "Would it have mattered?"

"Nah." He shook his head. "Should it?"

"Nah," she said imitating him. "But the lake ranger's house is down near the public entrance. Why aren't you living there?"

"The place needed renovations. The last ranger kind of let things go. After living there for a while, I made a deal with the town to have some work done. I pay for this one while they fix that one. And in my spare time I do as much of the work myself as I can."

"Ahh. Well, since you only need a temporary place, I'm sure Danny can find you something suitable."

He gave her a funny look. "This place suits me fine."

"But I'm back and I want my house."

"I have a lease."

"For how long?"

"Longer than your vacation."

"I'm not here on vacation."

He jacked an eyebrow. "What does that mean?"

"I've moving back."

An odd fire backlit his green, green eyes. A fire Kat could not interpret. "As in permanently?"

The familiar ache of indecision started up inside her head. She rubbed at her temples, confused and uncertain. Dr. Kathryn Elizabeth Thatcher was a highly skilled doctor who made decisions about other people's lives all the time. Why couldn't she figure out what to do with her own?

"Let's just say I'm here for some much needed R and R while I figure out some things."

"That's what I figured. So why not stay with Susan?"

Why did everyone keep asking her that? "Remember the old saying that fish and friends stink in three days? I've been there four."

Though she'd slept through most of them.

"Then ask Danny to find you a place."

He was starting to tick her off.

"Seth," she said as reasonably as possible. "I have a place. This place. Want to see the deed?"

"Want to see my lease agreement?"

"Why are you being so stubborn?"

"Why are you?"

"This is getting us nowhere." With a huff, she jumped out of the chair and stalked to the long row of windows, gazed out at the breathtaking view for a moment and then turned to try again. "I'll pay the rent on another cabin of your choosing."

"I like it here."

"I don't remember you being this difficult."

His jaw twitched and the fiery glint returned. "Time and experience changes a man, Kat. I've learned to fight a lot harder for the things I want."

Surely he wasn't referring to their long-ago relationship. They hadn't seen each other for years, and the man had married someone else.

"It's only a house, Seth. You can find another."

"That's what I keep telling *you*. Now if you don't mind . . ." He let the sentence trail away in cool dismissal.

"You're not going to give me back my cottage," she said incredulously.

"Nope. I'm not." He opened the front door and stood to one side. "Bye Kat. See you around."

What else could she do? With one final, scathing glance, she gathered her dignity and left.

With a mix of admiration, amusement and regret, Seth watched Kathryn stalk off through the woods, straight brown hair swaying against her shoulders, long lean legs churning the ground with purpose.

That was Kat. Always on the go, always filled with purpose and aware of exactly what she wanted. A long time ago she'd wanted him, but she'd wanted to be a doctor much, much more.

He shook his head at the thoughts. He hadn't seen Kathryn Thatcher in years. What did he know of her now?

Nothing. Not one thing other than she was still as pretty as an Easter lily and still had the uncanny ability to make him want to take care of her.

For one minute there, after he'd lowered the Glock 44 and while she gazed at him with shock and fear, he'd wanted to take her in his arms. For comfort purposes only, of course.

Kat. He hung his head for a moment and contemplated the wooden porch. Long ago he'd dealt with losing his first love, but seeing her again stirred some deep and elemental longing to set things right. They'd left a lot of business unfinished.

His conscience began to nag.

Finding Kathryn in his kitchen had been a shock he hadn't been prepared for. He'd come in, guns blazing like some Wyatt Earp cowboy and scared her to death, but that hadn't been enough for the big-city cop. Oh, no. He'd had to intentionally bait her about the cottage, too. He still hadn't figured that one out yet.

He studied his reaction for a minute, wondering if, in some juvenile way, he wanted to hurt her. He didn't. She had been hurt far more than he by their carelessness as teenagers. After the baby, they'd drifted apart, too guilt-ridden and ashamed to discuss what they both must have been feeling. He hadn't understood the reaction then. All he'd understood was Kat's abandonment.

He didn't blame her for that. Maybe he once had, but not now. Interesting how fifteen minutes with Kat had resurrected a memory he'd buried for years.

From the local talk, he knew she had never married, never had more babies. He had. God had blessed him in a thousand ways, even if Rita had killed him and their marriage with her infidelity.

As a Christian he should have been able to make his marriage work, but he'd failed somehow. Failed Rita. Failed his daughter. Most of all he'd failed God, but he didn't know what to do about it. Rita had been the one to file for divorce, and as hard as he'd tried to stop her, she'd divorced him anyway. Nothing much a man could do about that, Christian or not.

But in truth, their marriage had died long before the courthouse funeral. That was the part that haunted him.

Seth looked up, saw that Kat had disappeared from sight. Twilight hovered over the thick trees like a million black gnats.

Slowly he shut the door and went inside, chest heavy with emotion. Seeing Kat again had brought back all the questions.

He was thirty-six years old, divorced, alone, and still asking God why he'd been allowed to love two women in his life but hadn't been enough to keep either of them.

CHAPTER THREE

Kat slammed into the house, flip-flops thwacking against the gleaming hardwood floors. Susan had some explaining to do.

She couldn't believe Seth Washington was living in her house. Seth. Of all people. Why hadn't someone warned her?

She found Susan in the den, wrapping a gift for a baby shower at church. Her brother-in-law, golden-haired Danny, lay kicked back in his brown leather recliner watching a baseball game. Little Sadie, a dark-haired surprise in a very blond family, sprawled across her daddy's lap feeding him roasted peanuts. Ten-year-old Jon played some kind of hand-held video game while Queenie the pregnant cat followed his rapid movements in fascination. Shelby was nowhere in sight and Kat figured the fourteen-year-old was upstairs talking on the telephone. Her sister's family was about as all-American as they came.

When Kat entered the den, Susan glanced up with a smile.

"Hand me a blue bow, will you, Kat?" She indicated the coffee table and a plastic bag filled with a rainbow of colored gift bows.

Plastic and acetate rustled as Kat retrieved the needed decoration. Normally she'd ask about the gift, but right now she had more important things on her mind.

"Why didn't you tell me Seth Washington had rented my cottage?"

Her sister carefully creased the ends of baby-print paper and taped them down before speaking.

"I wondered where you had gone off to."

Kat clapped the bow into Susan's out-stretched hand. "He almost shot me."

Susan froze, hand still outstretched. The recliner mechanism popped loudly as Danny sprang upward. "What?"

She told them about the incident, finishing with, "As soon as he recognized me, he lowered the pistol, but he scared twenty years off my life."

"Seth's, too, no doubt. What on earth possessed you to go into the cabin?"

"It was one of those spur-of-the-moment things. And the cottage *is* my house." But she was feeling more foolish with each passing minute. Her quick decisions in the E.R.

were always right on. Snap judgments in life weren't quite as successful.

Susan's usual smile was replaced with a frown. "You worry me sometimes, Kat. All those brains and not a lick of sense."

Kat bristled at the taunt her family had thrown at her all her life. No one had said it in years.

"Susan," Danny chided gently. "That's not fair."

Susan's shoulders slumped. "You're right. I'm sorry. I should have told you about Seth."

At her sister's sweet apology, the tension dissipated but the words hovered in the back of Kat's mind, painful because she feared they were true. "Yes, you should have, but going into the house *was* stupid. I should have realized nothing good could come of it."

"But you did see Seth again — finally. I know how you've dreaded that initial contact."

Susan was right — again — though Kat didn't like being so transparent. "I wasn't exactly dreading anything. I've just been too busy to seek out a virtual stranger from the past."

Too busy sleeping and avoiding life.

Susan gave her a look that said she didn't

believe a word, but she returned to her package without argument. "So how does he look to you?"

Kat wasn't about to mention Seth's stunning green eyes rimmed in spiky black lashes or how the little creases beside his mouth, deeper now, still made her stomach flutter.

"Medically, he seems healthy enough."

Danny made a choking sound as he settled back into his recliner. "Talk about taking the wind out of a man's sails. I hope Seth never hears that summation."

Kat started to make some smart remark about men all being the same as long they had health insurance, but she figured her cynical outlook wouldn't be appreciated.

"I asked him to move out of my house."

Susan zipped off a strip of Scotch tape. "Don't you think that's a little selfish? Come on, Kat, if you don't want to stay here, there are other places to live until Seth moves into the ranger's house."

"I have a couple of vacant cottages that aren't booked if you're interested," Danny offered. "You've always liked that secluded little cabin near Dock Nine. We've been doing some renovations, but the place is livable."

He didn't bother to mention what Kat

already knew. The cabin was a stone's throw from her own A-frame, the one occupied by her former beau. If she moved there — something she'd have to think about — seeing Seth occasionally would be inevitable.

Oh, what was she thinking? If she stayed in Wilson's Cove for any length of time, she was bound to run into him now and then.

Fine. She could handle seeing Seth Washington. What happened all those years ago shouldn't matter now. Don't talk about it. Don't think about it and everything will be fine.

Susan came around the table to where Kat had plopped onto the fluffy faux-suede couch to think. She set the pretty wrapped package between them.

"We could sew new curtains and maybe slipcovers for the furniture. Fixing the place up could be fun. What do you say, sis? The Thatcher sisters together again, like old times."

Like old times. She and Susan had once been joined at the hip, but in the past ten years, Kat's work had stolen their time together. She'd thought she was the only one affected, but Susan had missed her, too. A powerful homesickness welled inside along with the bald truth that she was wrong to expect Seth to move out of the cabin just because she had come back to Wilson's Cove.

Maybe Seth had been more right than she realized. Maybe she *was* a snooty girl.

And she'd tell him so the next time they crossed paths.

Three days later, Kat, dressed in blue shorts and white T-shirt, knelt on the back deck of her slightly dilapidated new rental potting scarlet geraniums and contemplating what to do with the rest of her life. If she'd thought time spent here in Wilson's Cove would take away the emptiness inside, she'd been sorely mistaken. She felt as adrift and lost in this place of her upbringing as she had in Oklahoma City.

So often she wished her parents had lived longer, though Susan had always been her confidant. Still, a mother's shoulder and wise counsel, even to someone as old as she, sounded good right now.

Yet she hadn't leaned on her mother when she'd needed her most. She hadn't leaned on anyone but herself. She'd made the mess and she'd been determined to deal with it on her own. She'd hidden her secret well, too. No one had ever even suspected that the quiet, church-going Thatcher girl had gotten pregnant.

She sighed and shook her head. Why had all these memories started to torment her again?

Maybe she was clinically depressed. The question was why?

She was a successful, well-respected physician. She had friends. She had things. She had money. Why did life feel like one big disappointment?

Holding a single geranium upright in a small pot, she dug the fingers of one hand into the cool, moist potting soil. Susan insisted that flowers around the cabin would add character to the place.

If she knew her sister, planting flowers was intended as therapy for her as well.

The rental was smaller and older than her A-frame but neatly furnished with all the necessities. The property also boasted an old fishing dock right on the lake, though Kat didn't feel too confident about the dock's stability.

At some recent time Susan had added her touch to the bedroom, dappling on wall paint to create the look of faux leather. The pale tan was more suitable to a weekend fisherman, but the decor would do until Seth moved into the ranger's house. Whenever that happened.

The best thing about finding a new place

to live was that the activity took her mind off her real problems. She'd finally turned her cell phone on this morning and discovered twenty-three messages from the medical director. He wasn't the least bit worried, or so he said, about the frivolous lawsuit, and he'd cover her shifts for a few weeks until she was ready to come back. The leave of absence was just that, he insisted, a leave. He refused to believe she'd even consider resigning. He was wrong.

"Take a break. Get some rest," Dr. Beckham said when she had dialed him up. "Then get your tail back to work. We need you."

They'd haggled for twenty minutes, but he'd been adamant, and in the end she'd agreed. In all honesty, she didn't want to consider going back, though she hadn't told the director as much. She shuddered in dread at the thought of facing another ambulance filled with broken bodies while some ambulance-chasing lawyer stood in the waiting area ready to file suit because she wasn't God.

Whether here or there, life stunk.

"You look serious."

At the sound of that familiar gravelly voice, Kat jerked around and nearly lost her balance. At the sight of Seth Washington, she nearly lost her breath.

Lean and fit in his blue-gray ranger's uniform, dark hair glistening in the sunlight, Seth sauntered across the lush green grass. Susan was right. He looked good in that uniform.

Kathryn patted dirt around the droopy little flower before rising to her feet. "You have a habit of sneaking up on people."

"Haven't you heard? Good cops walk softly and carry big guns." Seth propped an elbow on the wobbly wooden porch railing, his eyes hidden behind dark sunglasses, his grin doing funny things to her concentration. Not that she was concentrating on anything too earth shattering.

"Still mad?" he asked.

For effect and to stop the crazy thoughts running through her head, she glared at him. "Yes."

After a beat of silence she laughed. "Not really. I just wanted to see your reaction. In fact, I want to apologize."

He arched a very dark eyebrow. "For?"

"Breaking and entering. Conduct unbecoming. Rude behavior."

"You were surprised. No big deal."

"You were surprised, too, but you didn't get angry."

"No, but I pointed a loaded gun at you.

That would make me a bit testy."

"Stop being easy on me. I was a brat and I'm sorry."

"You've always been a brat, but I like you, anyway."

He'd said *like* as in the present tense. Could he really not hate her?

"I came to apologize to you," he said. "I was rude."

He made himself at home on her steps, crossing his ankles and leaning an elbow on the rough planks. A cell phone dangled at his hip instead of a weapon and a shiny badge glinted over his shirt pocket. He looked relaxed and comfy, a lot like the teenage boy she'd once known.

"Does that mean you're willing to give me back my cabin?"

He made a noise, half chuckle, half scoff. "Nope. 'Fraid not."

"That's what I figured. Go away." But she smiled when she said it.

"Can't do that, either." He removed the dark glasses and hung them on the edge of his shirt pocket while he studied her with a thoughtful gaze. "I really do want to apologize. I had no right to be rude to an old friend."

"Apology accepted."

"So does that mean we can be friends again?"

Friends? Could she be friends with a man whose presence brought back the most agonizing time in her life?

The memory rose between them, hovering like a red wasp waiting to sting. Did he feel it, too? Or was she the only one who still battled the guilt?

Maybe men weren't affected in the same way a woman was. Maybe he'd moved on and forgotten. Maybe he'd never been filled with the same sense of guilt and shame.

And just maybe the time had come for her to stop thinking this way.

An expert at compartmentalizing, Kat pushed the thoughts down deep. She would always care about the boy she'd known in high school, but she wouldn't open the painful Pandora's box that had been their relationship.

Still she wanted to know how he'd been, if he'd been happy, if all his other dreams had come true.

"I heard you were divorced." The thought, half-formed, had become words before she could think better of saying them.

He blanched, and some of his ease disappeared. He stared out at the serene lake, his face in profile, serious and rugged and maybe even a bit tragic.

Kat wished she'd kept her mouth shut. No one walked away from a divorce unscathed.

After a painful beat of silence in which Kat tried to think of a way to take back her unfortunate words, Seth released a gusty breath. "Two years later I'm still in shock."

"Unfortunately, divorce happens." All the time, from what she'd seen, but she felt bad that a broken home had happened to Seth. He'd suffered enough of that as a teenager.

"Not to me. I don't believe in divorce. I hate it, hate even saying the words."

So Susan had been right. "So I guess that means the split wasn't your idea."

"No." The word was flat and hopeless. "Not my idea, but probably my fault. Cops don't always make the best husbands."

"I'm sure you did the best you could." The words were platitudes even to her ears.

"I did. That's the agony of the thing. We had a Christian home, a Christian marriage. Or so I thought. All the time, Rita was going through the motions, playing church but seeing someone else on the side. I was a fool without a clue. Not a single clue until I came home from shift one morning to find her lover drinking coffee in my kitchen. They wanted to tell me together."

48

Emotion darkened his light-green eyes to the color of grass. His ex-wife had wounded him terribly. No surprise there. Seth was the sticking kind. The surprise was that he'd become a Christian.

Instinctively, as she often did with patients, Kat reached out and placed her hand over his. Seth's skin was warm and masculine tough against her fingertips. "What an awful thing to do to you. I'm sorry, Seth. Truly."

"Me, too, Doc." He gave her a lopsided grin and carefully slid his hand from beneath hers and rubbed at his smooth-shaven jaw. The action was intentional, Kat was sure, his way of letting her know that he did not welcome her touch. "But a broken marriage is something even a good doctor can't fix."

"I know." She folded her fingers into a fist.

This was the frustration of being a doctor. No matter how hard she tried, she couldn't fix everything. And there were always people who couldn't accept that fact, including her.

Her visitor gave the porch railing a shake. The old wood wobbled like a bobble-headed doll.

"I can, however, fix this for you." He nodded toward the rickety old fishing dock projecting out into the lapping water. "And that, too."

"Feeling guilty about stealing my house?"

"Maybe a little, though dock inspection and repair is part of my job. Safety on the lake, first and foremost. Fix it or tear it down."

"Doesn't matter to me." Nothing much did these days. "I really don't care one way or the other."

"The next renter might. I'll fix it." He slid the sunglasses back into place. "You sound a little down. Everything okay?"

Like she was going to tell him all her troubles. "I'm fine."

He didn't look as if he believed her but he had the grace not to say so. "Well, I guess I better get moving. There's always work to do on the lake."

"Not to mention the fact that you're the only thing resembling law enforcement in Wilson's Cove."

"That, too. But I don't mind. Policing both the town and the lake was part of the deal when they hired me. I'm more cop than I am lake ranger, anyway."

"The county sheriff has always taken care of Wilson Cove."

"That was before the lake grew so popular. Sheriff Trout has an entire county to cover with four men."

Not to mention he was stationed thirty miles away in Henderson. "Any luck with finding out who's responsible for the recent break-ins?"

"Not yet. Nothing's been reported for a couple of weeks so maybe the perps were short-term visitors. But just in case, keep things secured and be alert."

She'd worked in an inner city for years. A physician knew about secure and alert.

She tilted her head in a teasing smile. He sounded so incredibly macho. "Will do, Officer."

"I mean it, Kathryn. You're a woman alone. If you should need me . . ."

"I know where you live." She couldn't resist saying, "In my house."

Some of his seriousness left and he shook his head in amusement. "Still the same sassy mouth." He slapped the top of the railing, said, "And I'll be back to work on the dock as soon as I can."

She'd try not to be here. She didn't say that, either. But being near Seth resurrected too many memories. She was depressed enough as it was.

"Thanks."

"So, I guess I'll see you at church on Sunday?"

51

"Church?" Her conscience pinched. She hadn't been to church in years. Hadn't even thought about going.

"Does that surprise you? That I go to church now?"

She tilted her head to one side. A robin swooped to the ground beside the porch and nabbed a worm.

"A little."

"All those times you talked about your faith finally soaked in," Seth said. "I took a while to get the message, but the first time I looked down the wrong end of a nine millimeter and came out alive, I promised God then and there to follow Him. I wouldn't have survived the last couple of years without Him."

One of the few things they'd fought about as teens was Seth's lack of a relationship with God. Somewhere along the way, while she'd been losing her faith, Seth had discovered his.

The irony wasn't lost on Kathryn, but it was a bitter pill to swallow.

The gentle breeze stirred, sending a lock of hair into her eyes. Her hands were so dirty, she left it.

"So what do you say?" Seth pushed the curl aside and leaned in, green eyes aflame, lips tilted. "See you Sunday morning? Ten-thirty? If you're nice, I'll let you sit by me."

The brush of his hand against her cheek warmed Kathryn more than the seventy-degree day. And that was neither good nor acceptable. She backed away, breaking contact as he'd done earlier.

"I appreciate the invitation, Seth. Really. But I won't be coming to church."

A slight frown puckered his dark, slashing eyebrows. "Why not? Don't want to sit by me? Or are you already heading back to OKC?"

"I don't know an easy way to say this." A knot formed beneath her breast bone, like a hand squeezing her heart, but he might as well hear the truth directly from her so he wouldn't be asking. "I don't go to church anymore, Seth."

He stilled, alert and watchful. "Care to explain that a little better?"

Explain? How did she explain what she didn't understand herself?

Even through the sunglasses, his gaze bored into her, earnest and concerned. She didn't want his concern. She didn't want anything from him.

Turning her head, she stared out over the silvery lake. In the far corner of a nearby cove, a single boat bobbed above the gentle current. The soft murmur of voices, sprinkled with laughter, carried across the water. The scene was a happy one. Serene. Peaceful.

Kathryn couldn't feel that peace, hadn't felt peace in a long time.

"Somewhere along the line I lost my faith," she said to the wind, though she could feel the intensity of Seth's gaze burning a hole in her conscience. "I wish I still believed that God was the answer to everything. I wish I believed He cared. But the truth is, Seth," she said, swinging her gaze to finally meet his, "I don't believe in anything at all."

CHAPTER FOUR

Lost her faith. Kat's bald statement rolled round and round inside Seth's head as he drove along the lake's edge checking for problems and then into town.

Kat no longer believed in God? He couldn't take it in. All through high school her Christian stand had impressed him. So much so that he'd carried the seed of her witness to Houston and ultimately to a relationship with the Lord.

What could have happened to steal Kat's faith?

A sick foreboding started low in his belly and climbed, full grown, into his mind.

He pulled the truck into the slanted parking spot in front of O'Grady's Hardware Store and killed the motor. Hands gripping the steering wheel, he squeezed his eyes closed and huffed a painful sigh.

Today he'd gone to Kathryn's to apologize and maybe to be a friend. He wanted nothing else from her. In fact, he never wanted anything from any woman again except friendship. Not with his track record. Somehow he'd destroyed his marriage and let God down. And a long time ago he'd failed Kathryn.

The reckless kid he'd been back then had blamed her as much as himself. Maybe more. She was the one who had ultimately walked away, who wanted a career in medicine more than anything else, including him. He'd resented that so much.

But now he wondered. Had the wounds they'd inflicted on each other caused her to question God?

The only sensible answer was yes.

He was the reason Kathryn no longer believed. Because of what he'd done, what he'd caused her to do, seventeen years ago.

"Lord, I could use a little guidance here," he murmured. "I've messed things up again."

He made the same confession a lot lately.

When his prayer brought no immediate answer, he exited the truck, habitually snicking the locks. Half the people in Wilson's Cove still didn't lock their cars or houses, a worrisome practice he was trying to change.

For the most part, the sleepy little town experienced few crimes and the townsfolk were convinced no one would steal from them personally. Summer people, they claimed, caused all the trouble, pointing to the rise in problems from Memorial Day to Labor Day. After years of working the streets of Houston, Seth might be cynical, but safety first was not a cliché.

As he stepped up on the sidewalk, he was greeted by passersby who called him by name and asked how he was doing. This was one of his favorite things about moving back to Wilson's Cove. Here he had a name, a dozen people he called close friends and many more acquaintances, folks he'd known all his life. Though years and miles had separated them, the town embraced him again as soon as he declared his intent to stay. He'd never leave here again, ever. He was home and this was where he wanted to live out his life. Nothing could drag him away again.

His single status was the object of the town's gossips, but he didn't mind much. In a town this size, talking about each other was the major source of entertainment. As long as the conversation remained truthful, no one was hurt. Anyway, that was his way of thinking.

He appreciated the motherly ladies, too, who handed him foil-wrapped lasagna and slices of homemade pie or invited him to dinner after church each Sunday. Many of them had known his mother during the hard times and seemed to enjoy spoiling Virgie Washington's boy. Life was good here in Wilson's Cove, and as the only law-enforcement official for miles around, Seth planned to keep it that way.

This was one of the reasons the break-ins worried him so much. Four in less than two months, all on weekends, which led him to suspect lake weekenders or their kids. Other than a few unidentifiable tire tracks and nonregistered fingerprints, he had exactly zero evidence.

As he scraped open the door to O'Grady's Hardware, Seth sniffed wood shavings and motor oil and a hint of this morning's coffee left on the burner too long. The scents were a step back in time. O'Grady's had been here as long as Seth could remember and sold everything from tools and car parts to wood stoves and burial policies. The latter had never struck a single soul as an odd thing for a hardware store to sell.

"What can I do for you today, Seth?" Jim Green, the mustached clerk, asked. The two men had gone to high school together and played on the football team. Even now, Jim was as big and burly as an offensive lineman. "Need more insulation for that ceiling?"

"Lumber today, Jim. I have a couple of docks to repair."

"The town's getting its money's worth out of you, isn't it?" Jim asked with a grin.

"I hope so. Wouldn't want them to fire me."

"No chance of that happening." Before Seth could swell with the compliment, Jim finished with, "Who else would take a job in this place?"

Maybe no one, but Seth was thankful for the opportunity just the same. If he'd stayed in Houston, he wasn't sure what might have happened. He'd definitely lost his edge after the divorce, one thing an inner-city cop could not afford to do.

He handed the man his list and began to move around the store, picking up the things he needed while Jim took care of the items in the lumberyard.

He was standing next to the paint samples, a can of weather retardant in one hand when the old door of the hardware store, swelled with spring humidity, scraped open against the concrete floor. Seth glanced up as Susan Renfro entered. She spotted him immediately.

"Hey, Seth. I thought that was your truck

out there. How ya been?"

"All right. You?"

"Fat and sassy." She laughed and stepped up to the racks of paint swatches. "Emphasis on fat."

Seth smiled. He'd always liked Kat's sister, and even though she'd gained a few pounds, he thought she was still one of the prettiest women in the Cove. "I saw Kat this morning."

Her grin turned to curiosity. "Really? I don't see any blood. Didn't she whop you upside the head for renting her cabin?"

"I think she's over being mad. At least, I hope she is." He picked up a paint stick, adding the wooden paddle to his collection of odds and ends. "She told me she doesn't go to church anymore."

Susan studied a paper strip with varying shades of brown. "Not in a long time. I'm surprised she told you."

"Guess she didn't have much choice. I asked if she'd be at church Sunday."

Kat's sister arched a brown eyebrow. "Bet that went over well."

Not particularly. He'd felt the invisible wall rise between them as soon as he'd asked.

"What's that all about, Suz? Kat's faith is the reason I'm a Christian today. How could she stop believing?"

"I wish I knew. She went off to college and the next thing I know, she's refusing to attend church." She frowned. "Come to think of it, she stopped going to church before leaving for college."

That's what Seth was afraid of. His stomach fell to the toe of his boots and stayed there. Here was his answer. Kat had left the faith because of him. Rita had claimed the same thing. She even said she'd faked being a Christian to make him happy. He, Seth Washington, had caused two women to lose trust in God.

Wasn't he special?

Susan thrust a strip of pale browns beneath his nose. "Which of these do you like best?"

What did he know? Brown was brown.

"That one," he said, putting his finger on a medium shade in the center of the card.

"Terrific. I like chamois, too."

Chamois was a color? He'd thought it was a cloth for polishing his truck.

While he pondered that bit of information, Susan switched gears on him. "We need to help her."

"Who?"

She looked at him as though he'd been struck with a sudden onset of attention deficit. "Kat, of course."

His belly did that sinking thing again.

He was all for helping people. To serve and protect, that was his motto, but he wasn't sure Kat would appreciate the interference. "How?"

"She's depressed. Didn't you notice? I guess I shouldn't be telling you this, but I thought . . ." Her voice trailed off, though Seth figured he knew where she was heading. And he didn't much like the direction.

"I noticed she seemed down." Kat had lost her sparkle, her confidence.

"She is. She's being sued for some stupid thing and thinks she wants to leave medicine for good."

Seth held back a disparaging sound. "She won't do that."

He knew better. Kat wouldn't give up the career she loved. She wouldn't stay in Wilson's Cove. She might be tired and need a vacation among hometown folks, but that's all it was — a vacation.

"I don't think so, either, but I'm worried about her." Susan raised a yellow color sample up to the light. "Why don't you come for supper tonight and we'll talk?"

Talk? About Kat? No, he didn't think so.

The hardware clerk, sweat on his upper lip, traipsed down an aisle toward them.

"Got your stuff together, Seth. Pull around in back when you're ready."

"Will do. Add these to the tab, will you?" He handed off the armload of supplies and waited for Jim to start back to the register before saying to Susan, "I'm not sure Kat would be happy to be the topic of this conversation."

"Kat's not happy about anything, anyway."

But she was a private person who wouldn't appreciate her sister's interference. "Why are you telling *me* this?"

Susan lifted one shoulder. "Because she won't listen to me. She gets her back up whenever I mention God or church."

"That's too bad, Susan. Seriously, but I don't understand where I come into the picture. Kat and I don't even know each other."

"But you were once close."

Yes, too close. Close enough to break each other's hearts and change the course of their lives. He refused to let his mind go in *that* direction.

"I'm sure she has close friends today, probably even a boyfriend. Why not talk to them about this?"

"Number one," Susan tapped a paint card against her fingers as she ticked off the reasons. "Kat isn't currently seeing anyone.

Number two, I don't know any of her friends. And number three, you just expressed concern about Kat's lost faith. I thought you'd be interested."

Right. He *had* asked. And he *was* interested. He just wasn't sure getting personally involved was a good idea.

"It's only supper, Seth. You haven't been over in weeks. And if you don't want to discuss Kat, that's fine. We can have supper and a good visit. We'd love to have you."

"All right, then. Supper sounds good. I need to talk to Danny about a couple of old dilapidated cabins east of the marina, anyway. What time?"

"Shelby has piano after school. Let's make dinner around six, okay?"

"I'll be there."

A man had to eat, and Susan Renfro was the best cook in the county. Kat didn't have to be part of the equation. In fact, he'd make sure Kat was not part of the equation. There were some mistakes a man did not want to repeat.

He'd been set up.

Anyway, the casual evening at Susan's felt like a setup to Seth.

He'd been sitting in Danny Renfro's living room, enjoying a friendly argument about baseball. He liked Danny. Everyone did. Tall and so blond the guys in school had called him "surfer boy," Susan's husband had enough personality to sell raincoats in the dessert. His real estate success surprised no one, though he'd gotten a good start by marrying a girl whose family had once owned the lake and all the land around it.

Susan had been in the kitchen, creating something that smelled so delicious Seth's bachelor stomach whimpered in anticipation.

Thirty minutes into a relaxing evening, the front door opened and Kat walked in.

For a few seconds Seth was transported back to a time when he'd eagerly waited here in this very room for Kat to come bounding down the stairs, ready for a Saturday-night date.

More interested in books than being popular, Kat had never been a fashion diva, but she always looked good to him. Tonight she was dressed in capris — or whatever women called those short pants — and a pink shirt. She looked as she had in high school, fresh and pretty.

Her long brown hair was pulled back in a ponytail. Simple. Clean. Neat. Very like the girl he remembered. She was curvier now, a change he appreciated, though he probably shouldn't be noticing.

Back in high school, Susan had been Miss Popularity, the outgoing cheerleader type while Kat had stayed in the background, quietly plotting her future.

At the time, he'd expected that future to include him. Of course, it hadn't.

Young and cocky and in love, his heart had always accelerated the moment he locked eyes on her.

His heart accelerated tonight, but for different reasons. He wasn't quite sure, however, what those reasons were.

Kat, too, must have been taken unawares because as soon as she saw him, she paused. Only a beat, but he noticed.

The trip down memory lane was broken by that infinitesimal beat of time. This was not the Kat he'd known. And he was no longer that love-struck boy.

"Seth," she said. "I didn't know you were coming."

"Same here."

Kat looked from him to Susan who had appeared in the doorway between the kitchen and living room.

"Kat, honey." Susan, cheeks rosy from the heat, sounded a bit too chipper. "Come help me get supper on the table."

With that, she plucked Kat's shirtsleeve and guided her into the kitchen. Quiet, undecipherable conversation rose amidst the clamor of plates and pots and kitchen appliances.

"My wife up to something?" Danny asked.

The two men sat facing each other, the muted television flashing pictures of the evening news and weather. Danny held the remote in one hand, waiting for the sports report.

Seth gazed at the now-empty doorway. "I hope not."

"Don't hold it against her if she is. She means well. She worries about Kat."

"She told me."

"And you're wondering why she's dragging you into the fray?"

"Something like that."

"Can't say for sure, but I know this much. After their parents died in that wreck, Susan felt responsible for Kat, being the big sister and all. If Kat's not happy, Susan wants to fix the problem, make things right."

He remembered that about Susan. Any time he and Kat had had a disagreement, big sister had been the mediator trying to get them back together. She must have been bewildered in those last months when Kat and Seth drifted apart, too broken to repair.

"Then there's the history between you and Kat. Suzie's a romantic."

A shudder of dread ran down Seth's spine. He sat up straighter. "Spare me that."

"You're both single. Why not?"

None of your business, he wanted to say, but this was life in a small town. Everyone stuck his nose in everyone else's business.

"As you said, we have history. Friends, yes. Anything else, uh-uh." His lousy track record spoke for itself. "I'm sure Kat would say the same."

The woman in question chose that moment to come out of the kitchen. "Dinner is on. You guys wash up."

Susan stepped up beside Kat. Seth couldn't help noticing the differences in the two women were more than physical. An ever-present joy shone from Susan's blue eyes while Kat looked tense and a little sad.

Susan yelled up the staircase, "Kids! Supper. Sadie, put that cat outside." She pulled a face at Seth. "Sorry. Didn't mean to break your eardrums."

Seth grinned back. Susan was as likable as her husband.

After a trip to the sink, Seth joined the Renfros at the big family-style table. A feast was laid out before them.

"Seth, you sit here." Susan said, indicating a place beside the only boy child, Jon. Kat was already seated on the other side of the table with Shelby at one elbow and an empty space at the other. "I hope you like pork tenderloin and mushroom gravy."

He slid the napkin into his lap. "A man alone likes anything he doesn't have to cook or buy at a restaurant, but this looks and smells amazing."

Little Sadie climbed into the chair beside her aunt. Kat scooted the child closer to the table and, with an indulgent smile, handed her a napkin.

"Bow your heads, kids," Danny said and waited until the room was quiet before giving thanks.

Though glad for the food and the friendship, Seth ached with a renewed sense of loss. His own family, though much smaller, had once shared this same routine.

He opened his eyes to take in the picture of what a Christian family was meant to be. Kat sat, eyes open, staring down at her plate. She must have felt his stare because she looked up.

The old Kat would have winked or made a face. This one gave a cynical twist of her lips that made him sad.

After the prayer, an abundance of food moved in an orderly fashion around the table. Fresh radishes and wilted leaf lettuce from Susan's garden. Fluffy mashed potatoes and buttery hot rolls.

Conversation flowed around the table with the food, easy and comfortable. Talk of the lake, the town, the high school baseball team. Seth relaxed and joined in, as did Kat. The evening was turning out better than he'd expected.

In fact, he found himself waiting for the times when Kat would comment and listening for the things that made her laugh. Kat didn't laugh as much as she used to, but when she did, the sound was rich and throaty and came from her heart.

Kat had a big heart.

Or she once did. What did he know of her now?

And why couldn't he stop thinking about her, stop watching her, stop waiting for those times when their gazes collided? Susan and her innuendoes had gotten to him.

Eventually, the conversation turned to the break-ins, something he could sink his teeth into. Anything to stop thinking about the woman who'd jilted him.

"Any news on that front, Seth?" Danny asked.

Seth shook his head. The episodes were

troubling but not violent. Still, he wanted to see an end to them. "I sent the fingerprints from the Millers' house to the state lab, but there was no record found."

"Figures," Kat said. "If kids are responsible, their prints wouldn't be recorded in the state files."

"I think our vandals are weekenders," Susan added as she passed Seth another roll. "The trouble always happens on weekends."

Seth didn't bother to point out that kids had more free time on weekends, too, even though he tended to agree with her assessment that someone other than locals was responsible. Anyway, he hoped so.

"Jeremy Fisher's dad said he'll shoot anyone who tries to break in to the bait shop," young Jon said. "He bought a new pistol up in Henderson."

Seth glanced down at the boy with a look of concern. They didn't need a citizenry up in arms. Most folks in this part of the country owned at least one gun, mostly for hunting, but a lethal weapon nonetheless.

"I hope you'll discourage that kind of talk," he said to Danny. "It's dangerous."

Danny nodded. "I certainly will, but you have to know lots of folks are talking, not just Ken Fisher."

71

Seth knew all right, and the talk worried him.

He picked up a knife to butter his roll and said, "I was hoping to have this thing solved before Alicia arrives. Looks like that's not going to happen."

His daughter's visit was an amazing turn of events, considering the fact that he'd had to fight Rita for every visitation in the past. Now she was letting Alicia come to Wilson's Cove for the entire summer.

"Alicia?" Susan asked, a forkful of potatoes halfway to her mouth.

He nodded. "My daughter. She lives in Houston with her mother."

"And she's coming here?" The teenage Shelby's eyes lit up. "How old is she?"

"Fourteen."

"Cool," Shelby said, her braces flashing. "Way, way cool. I'm fourteen, too. Maybe we can hang out and I'll show her around."

The offer warmed him. Shelby was a nice kid. With her as a friend, Alicia would meet the right kids. "I'd appreciate that. Thanks."

"No problem. New people keep summer from being so boring."

Both her parents laughed. Seth grinned. He'd heard the "boredom" complaint from Alicia.

"I don't think anyone ever mentioned that

you have a daughter," Susan was saying.

"What?" He pretended shock. "The ladies at the Quick Mart missed out on a piece of information? I thought they knew everything about everyone."

The table chuckled again and conversation moved to the two sisters, Donna and Sharon who collected information in the same way other women collected recipes. If you wanted to know about sickness or funerals or new babies or romances, Sharon or Donna had the scoop.

Amused by the topic, Seth glanced across the table at Kat. Eyes down, she pushed her lettuce from one side of the plate to the other. She must have felt his gaze because she looked up. What Seth saw in her expression both puzzled and concerned him.

A few minutes ago, she'd been laughing. Now she looked stunned.

"Kat?" he said quietly. The others, in a friendly argument over the last hot roll didn't seem to notice.

She shook her head and forced a smile. But he was trained to read body language. He saw.

Something had disturbed her.

Was it him? Had his casually tossed comments about Alicia come as a surprise?

Hadn't she known he had a child?

73

He held her gaze as realization dawned.
She hadn't known.
And even after all this time, Kat still grieved.

CHAPTER FIVE

Seth had a daughter.

After a restless night, Kathryn awoke with that one thought in mind. All morning as she'd been puttering around the house looking for something to do, she kept thinking of that moment when Seth had mentioned Alicia.

The news should not have come as surprise. He'd been married for some time. Having kids was almost a given these days. But for some reason the knowledge that Seth had sired another child brought all the memories tumbling in upon her like an avalanche.

She never thought about that terrible episode of her life. Hadn't thought about it in years. What had happened was over, done and behind her. She'd moved on. Seth had moved on. They were both successful people with good lives. She'd gotten over the loss long ago.

Her frazzled state of mind and uneven sleep had nothing to do with their secret.

Then why was she shocked by the news that Seth had a daughter?

Maybe being back in Wilson's Cove was the problem. Memories waited around every corner. Some good, some bad. Then there was Seth. He not only looked better than ever, he was a great guy. Everyone in town raved about him.

Maybe she shouldn't have come.

Right. But where else could she go?

She picked up the certified letter she'd been reading and tapped the paper against her forehead.

Here was part of the reason she'd come home to Wilson's Cove and why she'd stay. She was tired of the rat race because the rats were winning.

Last night Danny had told her about several available business ventures. Wilson's Cove was growing and if she was smart, she could find a new business to throw all her energies into. That's what she needed. A new project, a sense of purpose here in her hometown surrounded by family and friends. Then the depression would lift and she'd be happy. At the moment, she felt restless and useless. A new project was just what the doctor ordered.

Pushing aside the rest of the day's mail, Kat opened her laptop and typed in the password to a medical site available only to licensed physicians. Research was her escape, her solace, her fascination. For the past couple of months she'd been studying necrotizing fasciitis, better known as "flesh-eating disease."

That was the exciting thing about the medical field. There was always more to learn, and researching took her mind off everything else.

She was deeply focused on a fascinating case, taking notes like mad, when the sound of a hammer broke through.

Sitting back, she rubbed her eyes, then glanced at the tiny clock in the corner of the computer screen. Unreal. She'd been at work for more than two hours.

The hammer rang out again and she pushed up from the chair and followed the noise. As soon as she stepped out on the back porch, she spotted him. Seth, dressed in an ancient pair of jeans and a white T-shirt stood in the warm sunshine working on the rickety old fishing dock.

In spite of the uncomfortable history between her and Seth, she'd enjoyed last night's dinner at Susan's, and if she was truthful, she'd liked catching up with Seth.

He'd told tales of being a street cop in Houston, some funny, some sad. Through the stories she'd gotten a glimpse of who Seth Washington had become.

And she couldn't help liking him all over again. After all, he wasn't to blame about what happened. She was. And if his presence brought back the guilt, maybe she deserved the punishment.

Going back inside the cabin, Kat poured them both a glass of tea and started out once more.

The warm sun blinded her and she squinted against the glare. Barefoot, she crossed the thick green grass — the tickle against her tender feet pleasant after years on concrete and tile — and started down the slight incline toward the dock.

As she drew closer, she watched the concentration on Seth's face, noticed the muscles of his shoulders bunch with effort as he yanked away a rotting board. From a physician's perspective, he was a fit and healthy male. From a woman's perspective, he was a ruggedly attractive man.

Seth spotted her approach and paused in his work, letting the hammer fall to his side. His face glistened with sweat.

"Didn't disturb you, did I?"

"Actually, yes," she answered.

He didn't look the least bit repentant. "Good. I was hoping you'd come out and play."

She laughed. "You call this playing?"

"Play is all in the attitude. Everything is fun if we think it is." He drew a shirtsleeve across his face. "Is one of those for me or are you drinking doubles?"

"Oh, here." She'd been so fascinated with watching him, she'd forgotten the purpose of her visit. What was wrong with her, anyway?

He took the glass and tilted it up. The muscles of his throat worked as he swallowed the contents in one long gulp. Condensation dripped onto his skin and trickled down. Kat sipped at her own tea, marveling at the difference in the way men and women approach something as ordinary as drinking tea.

Well, not all men. She had no idea if any of her medical colleagues could swallow a glass of tea in one long gulp.

Seth released a gusty, "Ahhh," and handed her the now-empty glass. "Nothing like sweet tea. Thanks."

"Would you like more?"

"Later would be good."

"Anything I can do to help out here?"

The question caught him by surprise but

he said, "Well, let's see." He twisted his upper body to peer around; the sweat-damp T-shirt stuck to the middle of his back. "You could drag the old wood over to my truck if you wanted to."

"Clean-up committee?"

"Something like that. You don't have to."

"I know." Having a purpose felt good. She'd been busy for years. Idle time had started to wear thin. "I want to. It's my dock, at least for now."

He didn't rise to the obvious debate over her cottage. "Better get some gloves. Old wood will give you splinters."

"Don't have any." Other than latex which wouldn't do her a bit of good in this situation.

Seth stripped his away. "Take these."

Though pleased by the offer, Kat shook her head. "I couldn't take your gloves."

"They're in my way. I'm going to be using the nail gun. Don't need gloves for that."

Kat didn't believe a word of it. But she took the soft leather gloves and slid them onto her hands. The inner warmth from Seth's skin felt uncomfortably intimate.

Perhaps she shouldn't have come out here. She didn't know why she had, other than the need to be busy.

But she'd offered and she wouldn't back down.

After a trip inside for shoes and to refill the glasses, she began clearing away the rotted lumber while the sound of Seth's nail gun punctuated the air.

As they worked, the sun warm and the lake lapping lazily against the shore, conversation flowed much more easily than she'd expected, almost as if they'd never been apart. Later, she'd wonder about that but not now.

They talked of the dock, the lake, new folks who'd come to live here in the years they'd been gone. Sharing a common history had its good points, too.

And if both of them were a little too careful about touching on certain subjects, wasn't that understandable? She wasn't sure why it mattered, but Kat was glad they could be cordial again.

She tossed a final armload of discarded lumber into the pile on Seth's work truck. "I'm going to have to abandon you soon."

As quickly as the words left her mouth, she wished them back. Abandon was not a good word to use with Seth.

But Seth didn't seem to notice. Balanced on his toes, he crouched on the dock fitting new boards into place. At her comment, he glanced up.

"Wimp," he teased. "Can't take the hard work?"

She made a face at him. "I have some business in Oklahoma City. As much as I don't want to go, I might as well get the trip over with this afternoon."

He pushed to a stand. "Long drive by yourself. Why not ride up with me?"

"You're going to the City too?" Folks on the Cove always referred to the state's capital as "the City."

He glanced at his watch. "Around three. I thought I mentioned that last night. I have to pick up my daughter at the airport."

Kat tried not to react. "I wouldn't want to intrude on your reunion."

"You wouldn't be intruding."

She shook her head and pulled off the gloves, handing them over. "I don't think so. But thank you for the offer."

If Seth understood her reluctance, he didn't show it, and Kat was glad. No use bringing up the fact that he had a daughter and she didn't.

He shoved the gloves into his back pocket and went back to firing nails. Kat stood for a moment watching him, wondering what she was doing out here with Seth Washington in the first place. She should be running in the opposite direction, not feeling drawn to him.

Wheeling away, she was halfway up the incline when Seth exclaimed and metal clattered against hollow wood. She whipped around.

"Seth?"

Grimacing, he stood on the dock cradling one hand against his body.

Kat broke into a trot. "What did you do? Let me see."

As she talked, she pried the hand away from his body. A nail was embedded in the skin between his left thumb and index finger.

"Stupid, stupid, stupid," he muttered through gritted teeth.

"Come in the house so I can get this out."

"Can you?" He was trying to be tough, but the skin around his mouth had gone white with pain.

"I'd be a pretty poor emergency room doctor if I couldn't."

"Oh, yeah. How could I forget?" He managed a grin. "Lead on, Doc."

She marched him into the cabin and directed him to a kitchen chair.

"Get some pliers and yank it out," he said.

"This may come as shock, but that's exactly what I'm going to do. After I make sure you haven't hit a bone or a major blood vessel."

"Seriously? No high-tech, fancy tool made specifically for idiots who shoot nails in themselves?"

Her lips tilted. "Good old-fashioned pliers will do the trick. Needle-nose if you have them."

"In the toolbox in back of my truck. I'll get them."

"If you do that, I'll see what antiseptic I have around here for cleaning."

"No problem. I have a nail in the hand not in the head." He started out, hand cradled against his chest. At the front door, he paused to frown back at her. "I won't need stitches, will I?"

He probably wouldn't but Kat didn't say so. Feeling ornery, she said, "Don't be such a baby."

While he was gone, she spread a towel on the table, then ran a pan of warm, soapy water and got some gauze pads in case he'd struck a bleeder, which she doubted. These injuries were generally pretty well tolerated.

Seth reentered the cabin and placed the pliers on the table with a thunk. "Will these do?"

"After I wash them. No telling where they've been."

84

"Picky. Fish guts won't hurt anything."

She rolled her eyes and waited for the pleasant sound of his chuckle. Seth was still a fun guy.

He sat patiently in the chair in front of her while she scrubbed the pliers. The wound must throb, but he didn't complain.

Kat pulled his hand into hers and studied the puncture site. "Clean shot, all the way through."

"Nail guns are powerful."

Gently, she turned his hand over. "You have blisters, too."

"No big deal."

Well, the blisters were a big deal to her. He'd gotten them because she'd worn his gloves.

Gingerly she pressed the swelling flesh around the entry wound. "Looks like you shot straight through the web. That's good. Nothing major is affected, but there's no easy way to pull out a nail. It's going to hurt a little."

"It already does." He held steady while she settled the pliers firmly against the base of the entry wound.

Bracing his hand against the table, she said, "Ready?"

Using his other hand to help hold his arm steady, he sucked in a breath and braced himself. "Go for it."

The task took effort, a steady pull against already insulted human flesh, but Kat wrenched the embedded nail free.

"Sorry." She glanced up at Seth's face. Sweat had popped out on his forehead.

"Ouch," he hissed through gritted teeth.

"A little clean-up and we're through."

"Thank you, Lord."

And he meant the quiet words, as if God was a friend sitting next to him. Kat almost envied his easy faith. She'd been that way once.

Using the four-by-four gauze pads, she cleaned his hand, swabbed the tiny puncture wounds on each side with antiseptic and then applied antibiotic ointment.

As she worked, they were inches apart, Seth's breath a moist warmth against her cheek.

She touched people all the time. Holding Seth's hand should have been a purely medical exercise. It wasn't.

She noticed the hard strength in him, the rough manliness of his skin, the blunt cut of hard fingernails.

"You still play the guitar," she stated as she found the telltale calluses on his finger-tips.

"Still play. Still play badly."

When she looked up, amused, he grinned into her eyes. Her pulse jumped. She released his hand and leaned away. "All done. When was the last time you had a tetanus shot?"

"I don't know. Maybe never?"

"You'll have to get one."

"Got one handy?"

She shook her head. "The closest place I know of is the E.R. in Henderson."

He glanced at his watch. "No time."

"Seth, you have to have a tetanus shot. Stop at an E.R. or a clinic in the City."

"Nah, I'll be okay." He pushed to a stand. "Unless you want to go with me and pick one up somewhere."

She plunked a hand on her hip. "Is that blackmail?"

"Ma'am, I'm a sworn officer of the court. Blackmail is an ugly word." He grinned. "But yes, that was blackmail. Either you give me my shot or I will die of lockjaw. I've heard it's a terrible way to die."

Her lips twitched with the need to laugh. "You always were incorrigible."

He looked incredibly pleased about that. "So what do you say? Are you going to save my incorrigible life?"

Kat disliked making the long trip to Oklahoma City alone. And she did need to see her attorney.

Oh, okay, she was enjoying this unexpected reunion with Seth. In her current state of mind, she could use the distraction. No big deal as long as they kept the past safely tucked away. And if her nerve endings tingled from having him near, she wasn't crazy enough to believe they meant a thing.

She rendered a dramatic sigh. "All right, then, I'll go with you. Although lockjaw might serve you right." When he laughed, she flapped her hands at him in a shooing motion. "Now get out of here so I can get cleaned up."

Seth wasn't sure why he'd insisted Kat ride along with him, but they'd been having fun in spite of the hole in his hand. Fool that he was, he didn't want the day to end.

Kat's wit was every bit as sharp, and her laugh as infectious, as ever. Unlike a lot of women, she didn't mind getting her hands dirty. A blue-collar guy like him appreciated that. Come to think of it, he'd always appreciated Kat. Even during those days when romance was on his mind, they'd also shared a vibrant friendship. He and the quiet, intensely brilliant Kathryn had genuinely liked each other.

He'd liked her then. He liked her now.

He glanced across the bench seat at his passenger. She'd dressed up, changing into a navy-blue skirt and crisp white blouse. And she'd pulled her hair up on the sides so that she looked neat and professional. Very businesslike.

This was a side of Kathryn he'd never known.

"This lawyer you're going to. Is he taking care of that lawsuit you mentioned?"

"She. My attorney is a woman." Blue eyes danced as though she enjoyed reminding him that women could be professionals too. "And yes, to answer your question, this is about the lawsuit."

"Are you worried? I mean, can they take your license or something?"

She shook her head and the long, straight hair whispered like silk against her shoulders.

"Nothing like that. A lawsuit of this kind only wants money, not justice. I'm just stubborn enough to expect justice instead of money. I didn't do anything wrong, and I want my name removed from the suit."

He was glad to hear her license wasn't in jeopardy. Kat's career was everything to her. Absolutely everything. Even though she denied as much, he couldn't help believing the lawsuit was the real reason for her leave of absence. She'd be back in OKC as soon as the problem was resolved and her equilibrium restored. He was as sure of that as anything.

"Will it happen? Can you get your name exonerated?"

"That's what I need to find out. My attorney has some things to go over with me, depositions and the like, and some papers to sign."

"Worried?"

"No. I'm mad and frustrated, but not worried." She turned in the seat, raising one knee slightly as she rotated toward him.

"Good. I know how important your career is."

"Not anymore, Seth. I'm getting out."

"Then why do you care if your name is cleared?"

She went silent, but he knew the wheels in her head were turning. He glanced at her profile. In the sunlight, her pale skin was so clear and soft-looking he had to fight the urge to touch her cheek.

"The principle of the thing," she said finally.

Seth bit back the temptation to say, "Yeah, right. And my name is Abraham Lincoln."

They drove along in silence for several

miles, eighteen wheelers ripping past, until Kat said, "How's the ranger's house coming along?"

"Trying to rush things so you can have your cabin back?"

"Of course." She grinned. "I told you I'm home to stay."

"Slow. Real slow. I could use some advice on wall colors and carpet and the like."

"Not from me. I have no taste. Susan's the decorator in our family."

"Who chose the things in your cabin?"

"Me."

"I like the way you put things together, the colors, everything. I'm serious, Kat. Don't look so shocked."

Kat had never had confidence in any area but her brains.

"Why don't you work on your house instead of my dock?"

"The dock is part of my job as the lake ranger. The house is on my own time."

"Which I hear you don't have much of."

"The gossip sisters again?"

"Among others."

He hitched a shoulder. "I keep busy. I like being active in the community and getting to know the people better."

As a matter of fact, the teams he coached, the classes he taught, the fishing tournaments he organized all gave him a sense of belonging. Other than holidays and summers with Alicia, his friends were now the closest thing he'd ever have to family.

That bitter pill pained him no end. He loved being a family man. Apparently, he was lousy at it. No use making the same mistakes over and over again.

"So are you happy here?" Kat asked. "Are you glad you moved back to the cove?"

"Absolutely. I'll never leave again. I miss seeing Alicia more often, but . . ." He let the thought drift away. No use complaining about what he couldn't change. "Life doesn't always turn out the way you plan, but God's been good to me."

Kat shifted toward him on the bench seat. No, she thought, life had not turned out the way she'd planned, either, and she couldn't understand why. She'd set goals, put in the endless hours of study and work, but she still felt empty.

"What's she like?"

"Alicia?" He smiled, his tough-cop expression softening. "She's trying to grow up. I don't like it."

"Daddy's little girl?"

"Yeah. And she has me wrapped around her finger. I know she does but I can't do a thing about it."

He loved his daughter. That much was clear and not a surprise. She'd known Seth would make a great father. Even when they'd been too young to have a baby, Seth had tried to be a man about it, at least at first. He was a born protector. She was the one who'd had other plans.

She felt as guilty about that now as she had then.

"I was the same with my dad," she said. "Susan and I both knew if Mom said no, we still had a good shot with Daddy."

"Does that mean you can help me avoid some of the pitfalls?"

"You're on your own, big guy. We women stick together."

He shook his head, eyes on the road. "Being a parent is a helpless feeling."

The statement was a spear to the gut. She'd been a parent less than three months, and Seth was right — it had been the most helpless time of her life.

CHAPTER SIX

Seth stood on one foot and then the other as he scanned the stream of passengers coming up the ramp at Will Rogers Airport. He was uncomfortable with the idea of Alicia flying alone, but both she and Rita had insisted Alicia was old enough.

To him she was still a little girl.

To make him more nervous, the flight out of Houston had been delayed due to a thunderstorm. He glanced at his watch. She was already fifteen minutes late.

He wished Kat was here so he'd have someone to talk to during the wait. In her practical, no-nonsense manner, she would tell him that planes were late all the time and that fourteen was plenty old enough to fly alone. She'd force a cup of coffee into his hands and tell him to chill out.

But at her request, he'd dropped Kat downtown at the attorney's office. From there she was taking a cab to the hospital and then to her apartment where they would meet.

He felt a little strange about seeing Kat's city home for the first time, though he had no idea why. He was already living in her other one.

"Daddy!"

Somehow above the buzz of voices and the clatter of luggage rolling over concrete, Seth recognized the sound. He whirled, and there was Alicia, barreling toward him, carry-on in tow, a bright smile lighting the way.

His heart lifted at the sight of his only child. Relief that she was on the ground and safe flooded him. Lord, he loved her.

She catapulted into his arms with a squeal of delight. "I missed you."

"I missed you, too, baby." He held her away from him. "Let me look at you."

She stepped back and cocked her head, one hand on her hip in a cutesy pose. Like half of the other teenage girls he'd seen today, she was dressed in a long, funky, belted top with skinny-legged pants and huge earrings. What was his baby doing wearing her mother's earrings?

"Wow." His little girl had gotten curvy and filled out in ways that he didn't want to think about. And if any other male so much as noticed, he'd have to pin their ears back. "Does your mom know you're wearing makeup?"

She laughed. "Dad, you're so silly. I'm *fourteen*."

He could see he had some adjustments to make. "Don't remind me."

Alicia replied with a roll of the eyes teenagers reserve especially for adults.

"I'm starving," she said. "All they gave us on the plane was like, three stupid pretzels. Who could live on that?"

"You were expecting, maybe, pizza?"

"Well, yeah."

He chuckled and took the handle of her carry-on. "Come on, let's get the rest of your luggage downstairs. Then we'll pick up Kat and go find some pizza."

"Who's Kat?"

They stepped onto the rumbling escalator.

"A friend who rode up with me from Wilson's Cove. She had some other things to do, too, so we'll meet at her place."

From her spot one step below, Alicia turned to look back at him with black-lined eyes. "Is she your new girlfriend?"

Girlfriend? Uh, no. How did he explain to his daughter that he'd figured out the hard way that he and women didn't jibe? Even if they did, Kat Thatcher wouldn't stick around the cove long enough to see the seasons change, much less to develop a relationship, no matter what she said.

"Kat's a doctor I knew in high school. She's getting a tetanus shot for me."

"Did you hurt yourself?"

He showed her the puffy, reddened hand and told the tale. By now, they'd reached baggage claim and quickly found Alicia's Pullman. The airport was small enough that they were out and on the road within a few minutes.

As they headed east toward downtown, Seth listened to his daughter chatter on about her life in Houston, her friends, her favorite music and the two boys between whom she couldn't choose.

Boyfriends. Yes, he had some adjustments to make.

When he could finally get a word in, he said, "I was surprised your mother let you come."

"Don't be. She and Neil wanted to take an anniversary cruise. And, as Mom said, three's a crowd." She tossed her hands into the air. "So here I am."

Ah. Well. Now he knew. Rita was off on a cruise. Usually such announcements about Rita and her new husband stabbed him through the heart.

For once he didn't feel a thing.

Kat stood near the front window, watching for Seth's emerald-green truck to pull into the parking space below. She'd given him the address and directions, but he wasn't familiar with Oklahoma City. She hoped he could find her in this winding residential area. As a precaution, he had her cell number.

She wondered how the reunion had gone with his daughter. He'd seemed a little uptight, though happy. From their conversation, she'd gotten the feeling that he thought his ex-wife was letting Alicia grow up too fast.

Most likely he was reacting in the typical dad fashion to a maturing daughter.

She shook her head and pushed the curtain wider. Thinking of Seth with a teenage daughter was quite a paradigm shift.

But if their child had lived, he or she would be even older.

A hot emotion rose in her chest.

Below, sun glared off a dark-green truck. Seth was here.

A trendy young girl hopped out of the passenger side.

The feeling in Kat's chest expanded. She

examined the emotion as she would a festering sore, shocked that the wound was raw after all this time. As a physician, she'd learned that spontaneous abortion was nature's method of ridding the body of a nonviable fetus. The event was objective, clinical and unemotional. A miscarried fetus was a parasite, not a baby.

Most of the time, she actually believed it.

Upon hearing the approach of voices, she opened the door and forced a smile. "Hello."

Seth made the introductions.

This was Seth's child, beyond any doubt. With his dark hair and green eyes and someone else's alabaster skin, Alicia was lovely.

"Come on in. How was your flight?"

"Boring." Alicia came deeper into the room, gripping a tiny shoulder bag against her side. She looked around with frank curiosity, her gaze landing on Kat's enormous entertainment center. "Cool apartment."

"Thanks."

"Mom and I live in a house," Alicia said. "The same boring house as before the divorce. Neil moved in when Dad moved out. I didn't even get a new room out of the deal. How sucky is that?"

Kat didn't know how to respond to such a

personal pronouncement and apparently Seth didn't, either. The poor guy blinked at his daughter as if she'd sprouted antennae.

"Well," Kat said to cover the uncomfortable silence. "Would you guys like something to drink?"

"We voted to go out for pizza," Seth said, with a grateful look. "How does that sound to you?"

Pizza with Seth? She really shouldn't, but her mouth said, "Terrific. However, you need that tetanus first. I have the syringe in the fridge. Make yourselves comfortable while I get it."

As she headed for the kitchen, Seth asked, "Did you get everything taken care of with your attorney?"

"I think so," she called. For now, anyway.

Alicia's loud whisper carried through the divider. "I thought you said she was a doctor. My doctor is old and ugly."

Kat suppressed a laugh and slammed the refrigerator door. There was a left-handed compliment if she'd ever heard one.

Syringe in hand, she entered the living area. "Yes, I'm a doctor, and here's proof. Your dad is getting a shot. Roll up your sleeve, Seth."

Seth shoved his shirtsleeve upward, holding the cloth at the shoulder. Alicia shuddered and looked on in morbid fascination as Kat quickly slid the needle in and out.

"All done," she said. "I've saved your incorrigible life."

Amused eyes glinted down at her. "Do I get a lollipop?"

"Sorry. We don't give lollipops anymore. Too much sugar."

"But I was a good boy. Don't I get a cool Band-Aid or anything?"

They were standing arm to arm, and Kat could feel the afternoon's heat emanating from his body and see the yellow flecks in his green eyes. An awareness shimmied through her. Cute. He was too cute.

"How about a stick-on tattoo?" she said, not wanting to end the banter.

Seth grinned. "Do you have SpongeBob?"

Alicia stared as if they both were too corny to live. She made a huffing noise and said, "Are we going for pizza or are you two going to stand there making goo-goo eyes at each other all day?"

Goo-goo eyes? Were she and Seth flirting? "Alicia!"

The girl threw a palm up. "Sorry." But her face was turned to the side and her body language said she wasn't sorry at all.

Kat stepped away. "I'll get my things."

Flirting. She and Seth had been flirting.

Had they both lost their minds?

Kat didn't see Seth or Alicia for several days after that, which was just as well. Busy exploring the limited business opportunities in and around the lake, she had already heard rumors amongst the townspeople that she and Seth were "seeing" each other. Ridiculous. But that's the way Wilson's Cove worked. Just because she'd ridden to Oklahoma City with Seth on business, the gossips were all atwitter. Poor, deluded souls.

All she wanted was to buy into a business or start a new one, anything to keep from going back to work at the hospital.

Armed with a list from her brother-in-law, she'd looked into purchasing an interest in the marina and considered franchises on both a fast-food restaurant and a fitness center. All were plausible possibilities though none excited her. And she longed to be excited about something again.

She was waiting her turn at the bank when a man and a woman approached her. The couple, Bill and Agnes Novotny, had been friends of her mother and father.

The plump, red-cheeked woman, husband in tow, bustled toward her with as much speed as her bulk would allow.

102

"Kathryn? Is that you? I heard you'd moved back. Honey, I'm so happy to see you. You are the spitting image of your mama. Isn't she, Bill?"

Kat laughed. Agnes had always claimed she resembled her mother and Susan her father. Neither was particularly true. "Agnes, hi. How are you?"

The two women exchanged brief hugs before Agnes flapped a hand and kept talking. "Oh, I have a twinge now and then from my old heart. You heard about that spell I had, didn't you? My lungs filled up with fluid until I couldn't hardly breathe."

Kat shook her head, but recognized the possible signs of congestive heart failure. The notion that her mother's friend was growing old and sick saddened her. "I've been away for a while, Agnes. I'm sorry to hear you've been ill."

"Well, I'm doing okay now, as long as I take my pills and don't get stressed out. It's not me I'm worried over. It's this silly husband of mine." Giant black purse dangling from one elbow, Agnes poked a thumb at the gentleman beside her. "Stubborn old mule won't go to the doctor. I was wondering if you'd look at a place on his arm."

"What kind of place is it?" Kat asked.

"Ah, it ain't nothing." Bill's sun-burnished

skin darkened with a blush of embarrassment. "Agnes makes a fuss over every little barnacle. I tell her it's a fact of life. When you get old, you grow barnacles."

"Just the same," Agnes fussed, pulling at his sleeve. Like most of the older farmers in the area, Bill wore long sleeves year round. "Mildred Pringle had a place come up on her neck that turned into cancer. Left the awfulest scar you ever seen. She's still taking them radium treatments. Doctor said the cancer spread to the inside and who knows what that stuff will do once it takes hold."

"Want me to have a look, Bill?" Kat asked. Most of the time when people asked for free medical advice, Kat was irked. But this was a dear, sweet couple who had fed her homemade kolaches and led her around their yard on a gentle old pony.

"See?" Agnes said to her husband. "I told you when we saw Kathryn standing over here that she wouldn't care one bit in the world to look at your arm."

"You sure you don't care?" Bill asked, shifting from one boot to the other. "A word from you would put Agnes's mind to rest. I don't want her having no more of those heart spells."

By now, Agnes had rolled her husband's

sleeve back to expose a large blackened mole on his forearm. One look was all Kat needed.

Frowning slightly, she said, "Agnes is right about this, Bill. You need to make an appointment with your doctor in Henderson and have this checked out."

"Is it cancer?"

"I can't say for sure without a biopsy, but the color and shape look suspicious."

Agnes hissed in a worried breath. "I knew it. I been telling him for weeks to let me call the doctor."

Bill made a face. "I don't know any of the new doctors over in Henderson. Last doctor I seen was Doc Perryman that time I fell off the barn and knocked myself silly."

Doc Perryman? The Cove's old physician had been gone for ten years.

"Time to find a new one, Bill," Kat said quietly. "Maybe Agnes's doctor will see you."

By now, Kat's turn with the teller had come, but she motioned the woman behind her to move foreword. Agnes and Bill were family friends, people she cared about. Getting Bill's arm biopsied was more important than opening a checking account.

She stared into the gray eyes of her father's friend, willing him to understand the seriousness without causing fright. She knew these old farmers. Tough and proud, they figured if they weren't in pain, they weren't sick. "Promise me you'll see about this, Bill."

"Can't you take the thing off for me? I'd pay you."

She smiled but shook her head. "I'm not practicing medicine anymore, and even if I was, my equipment is in Oklahoma City. A biopsy isn't something I can do in my kitchen with a paring knife." At Bill's disappointed look, she touched his arm. "I would if I could. Go to Henderson, okay? And let me know what you find out?"

"All right. I guess if you say so, I better get it seen about."

His wife's relief was obvious. She pulled Kat into a fluffy embrace and patted her back. "Thank you, honey. Your mama and daddy would have been so proud of you. You always was the smartest little thing."

"Let me know now," she reminded again as the older couple left the bank.

Agnes waved one hand over her shoulder and hurried Bill out into the sunny day and into the waiting sedan.

On the way back to her house, Kat thought about her old friends and made a mental note to follow up with a phone call.

If the mole on Bill's arm wasn't cancer, she'd turn in her medical license. With early treatment he would be fine. She simply had to be sure he got it.

As she turned down the short gravel drive to the cabin, Kat's stomach dipped. A shiny green Dodge truck parked at an angle along the edge of her yard. Seth was here.

She battled back a disturbing sense of anticipation. Rebuilding the dock was part of his job. He wasn't paying a social call. Nor did she want him to. Too much dark water had run under the bridge between her and Seth Washington. The teasing remarks in town had put silly thoughts in her head; that's all there was to this foolish rush of pleasure at knowing he was here.

Nonetheless, when she slammed out of her car and Seth looked up from beside the half-demolished dock, flashed a white smile and waved, she smiled and waved in return. Alicia lounged in a lawn chair on the side of the bank, reading a magazine, an IPod bud stuck in one ear.

After putting her groceries away, Kat carried a couple of sodas out to the dock. One side of the structure was mostly torn away and needed only a few more replacement boards. The other side and the base could take weeks.

Handing first Alicia and then Seth a can of cola, Kat said, "You've been hard at work for a while."

Seth sipped from his soda and then set the can aside. "A couple of hours I guess."

"And you haven't damaged yourself at all?" she teased. "I'm amazed."

"Not yet." He grinned and pushed back the bill of a black baseball cap. "I'm still waiting for my SpongeBob tattoo."

"They're on back order," she quipped. "How's the hand?"

"Barely sore." He stripped away his glove, holding the palm out for her examination.

She looked the area over but resisted the temptation to touch him.

"Healing nicely." Only a dot remained where the nail had pierced the skin.

"I had a good doctor."

Kat made a shushing sound. "Anyone could have done that, even without a medical degree."

"Maybe, but not everyone would have chased down a tetanus shot to save my incorrigible hide." His mouth quirked.

Kat rolled her eyes for effect. "Don't make me regret the decision."

The quirk became a full-blown grin. "Smart mouth." Taking a tape measure from his belt loop, he handed her one end. "Hold that against the end of this board, will you, and quit picking on me?"

Kat obliged, resisting the urge to stick out her tongue. Kidding around with Seth had always been fun. In the aftermath, she'd forgotten about that.

After finding the exact board length, Seth pulled a stubby pencil from his shirt pocket and marked the spot. Kat watched, fascinated. There was something about a man working with his hands that she found attractive.

"If you'll show me how, I'd like to learn to do this myself."

"No need. I'll get to it eventually."

"But I want to," Kat insisted. Although she'd never tried her hand at building anything, she loved seeing how things worked and putting them together. And if she did the work, Seth would have no excuse to come around making her like him again, reminding her of the unthinkable.

"Well, okay," Seth said, with a shrug. "Another person comes in handy sometimes. I'll show you what to do."

"Great. I can work out here when you're busy with other things."

"Trying to get rid of me?"

Kat gave a false laugh. "Of course not. But you haven't been around in a few days."

Not that she was counting.

Whether he believed her or not, he let the question pass. "I've been getting Alicia settled in, and then yesterday was Sunday. Church, you know."

He glanced up, eyes serious.

Kat refused to rise to the bait, but she could read his thoughts. Why wouldn't she come to church?

"Pastor Rich preached a good message from Jeremiah. It reminded me of the conversation we had the other day."

"What conversation?" she asked, and then wanted to bite off her tongue. If she'd wanted a sermon, she would have gone to church.

"The one about making plans. Jeremiah says God already has a plan for our lives, to prosper us, to give us a hope and a future. A plan that won't harm us. We just have to tap into His plan instead of our own."

Kat let Seth's words hang in the air unanswered. She knew she was miserable. She didn't need Seth or Susan or anyone else to insist her problem was spiritual. Being unhappy in her profession didn't have a thing to do with God or some eternal plan. Did it?

Rather than follow that line of thought, Kat turned her attention to Alicia. The girl had laid aside her magazine, unplugged the ear bud and was watching the adults with a curious expression. Kat scrambled for a new topic of conversation.

"How do you like Wilson's Cove so far?" she finally managed.

Alicia hitched a shoulder. Though over-dressed for Wilson's Cove, she looked trendy and cute and citified.

"Okay, I guess. The town is kind of small, but the lake is pretty."

"And very peaceful. That's why most people come here."

"Yeah, that's what Dad said. But mostly, peaceful translates to kind of boring."

Teenagers. Kat hid a smile. With that attitude Alicia would suffer a long summer. And so would Seth.

"I tried to convince her to go fishing off the back dock," Seth put in, his eyes sparkling with orneriness.

Alicia shuddered. "Ew. Nasty old fish smell? No thanks."

Seth laughed and the masculine sound made Kat shudder, too, though for a far more troublesome reason. She dragged her focus back to Alicia.

"Fortunately, Wilson's Lake offers other enticements. Swimming, boating, hiking, jet skis."

"Yeah, otherwise I really would die of boredom this summer."

"She's fixated on the fear of boredom," Seth said. He aimed a smile at his daughter. "You won't die, I promise. You'll have plenty to keep you busy. You've already made new friends. You could even get a job."

"Dad!"

Seth laughed again. Kat joined him.

Motioning toward a pile of new lumber, he said. "One of you grab a two-by-four and I'll show you how to measure and cut."

"I will," Kat said, eager to be active. "I take it *job* is a dirty word?"

Seth nodded. "Almost as dirty as boredom."

"I'm too young to work," Alicia said in aggravation. "Besides I met some pretty nice kids at church, and we're going to hang out. This one guy, Derek, is so cool. He even has his license."

The last sentence was spoken in near reverence.

Kat lifted an amused eyebrow at Seth.

"Derek Grimes," he said. "Good kid. Attends church. Active in the youth group."

"He's also the quarterback on the football team," Alicia said, dreamy-eyed. "Isn't that awesome?"

"Do I know him?" Kat asked.

Seth braced the measured board against a rock and reached for a Skil saw. Sliding on a pair of sunglasses, he briefly showed Kat how to operate the machine before saying, "Derek's mom and dad were a few years ahead of us in school, I think. Pat and Sheryl. Can't remember her maiden name."

"Oh, okay. I remember. Sheryl Saddler, I think." Kat didn't recall the boy but knew the parents. Nice people. "What do I do now?"

"Hold that end steady while I cut off the extra." She squeezed her eyes shut against the noise as he guided the saw steadily through the lumber. Sawdust danced in the air, filling her nostrils and sprinkling her arms. Now she understood why Seth had put on the sunglasses and was glad for her own.

Task completed, she dusted her hands together and stepped back. "What's next? Can't I be measuring or cutting while you do the hammering?"

He was on his haunches, fitting the freshly sawn board into the crisscross design. "I'd rather you hold the boards steady, if you're willing. When they're long like this, one hand isn't enough to ensure the placement is correct."

Well, she'd asked to learn. If learning

meant working in close contact to Seth, that was her fault for offering.

Kneeling on the edge of the dock, she steadied the lumber with both hands. Right away, she recognized her mistake. She was way too close to Seth. She could hear the slightly labored puffs of his breath and catch the weather-warmed smell of cotton shirt and working male. She shouldn't be noticing, but she was. Like driving at night through a construction zone, danger signs flashed in her head.

Maybe she should concentrate on Alicia.

Angling her body away from Seth, she said, "Have you met my niece yet? Shelby Renfro?"

Alicia looked as if talking to Kat bored her silly, but she said, "Yeah. Dad took me to her house the first day I was here."

Seth blasted nails down the new board, ending just above Kat's head. Another whiff of his cotton shirt tickled her senses.

"She's camped on Susan's doorstep every day since. That's why she's dying of boredom with me today. I didn't want her wearing out her welcome."

When he stepped away to rummage in a toolbox Kat pushed to her feet and moved to the edge of the dock. Better. Much safer with some distance between them.

"At Susan's?" she said. "Don't worry about that. Susan's place is Grand Central. She likes for the kids to hang out there."

"That's what she told me but I figured she was only being nice."

"Not Susan. She means it. Having everyone else's kids at her house is my sister's way of keeping tabs on her own. If she can see them, they're safe."

"Good policy." Frowning at a corner where two boards joined, Seth fired an additional nail. Though aware the noise was coming, Kat jumped. Seth noticed and grinned. She made a face at him.

"Let Alicia go there anytime. Really. Susan won't mind."

"See, Dad, I *told* you." Alicia flounced out of the lawn chair. "Shelby asked me to swim today. All of the kids will be there except me. Can I go *now?*"

Her tone was none too gracious, but Seth didn't react. "I'm too busy to drive you. You'll have to walk."

Alicia rolled her eyes. "Dad, it's all of about six feet."

In reality, the distance was more like six blocks. Around the lake everyone walked or bicycled most of the time, anyway.

Seth motioned with one hand. "Go. I'll

pick you up at four. Call if you need any-thing."

Alicia needed no further encouragement. With a final flip of one hand, she headed off in the direction of the Renfro house.

"How are things going with her?" Kat asked.

He shook his head as if he wasn't so sure. "Most of the time she's my sweet little princess. Then there are those other times when she's a smart-mouth stranger."

"A lot of young teens are that way. Grow-ing pains, I guess."

"She's been raised in church. She knows better."

Kat had been raised in church, too, for all the good it had done. "Was the divorce really hard on her?"

"At first she seemed okay. But now she has this crazy idea that her mother and I can somehow get back together."

"I thought her mother had remarried."

"She has! That's why the idea is ludicrous. But you know what Alicia said to me last night?"

"I can't imagine."

"She said since her mom divorced me, maybe she can divorce Neil, too. Then the three of us can be a family again."

"Oh, my." Poor Seth. Poor Alicia. A fantasy like that could only bring heartache.

"Exactly." Leaning his backside against the dock rail, he removed his baseball cap and slapped it against his thigh. "The weird thing is, I can relate to how she feels. When my parents split up, I was relieved to see the fighting end, but something inside me kept hoping they would both change and work things out."

"I remember." They'd been dating during that difficult time when his mother had finally gotten the courage to divorce his abusive father. Seth had become the man of the family, responsible for his mother's safety.

"Yeah, I guess you do. I dumped a lot of my stress on you, didn't I?"

"I didn't mind." She'd loved him. But his despair had deepened not only their love for each other, but their need, as well, a need that had eventually turned from comfort to out of control.

Seth must have been thinking the same thing because his gaze shifted away. He caught his bottom lip between his teeth and stared out at the glimmering lake. The painful memory pulsed between them as steady and insistent as waves lapping the shore.

They'd never talked about what happened. Not once. They'd simply drifted apart, both too stunned and ashamed to know what to say.

Maybe that was why the memory had come back with such a vengeance. Seeing each other again had brought back all the unfinished business.

Since the day Seth had pointed a pistol in her face, an ache had started deep inside her soul and not let up.

He slapped the cap back on his head. "I don't want my child to suffer for my mistakes."

Kat flinched inwardly, the ache rising to a crescendo. Mistakes. She'd made so many. She crossed her arms and lifted her face into the cool breeze blowing in off the lake.

At times she wondered if her child had suffered — and died — because of her mistakes.

Now she worried about making more mistakes. Leaving medicine. Starting a new business. Moving home to the cove. Even Seth was a mistake she could make all over again if she wasn't careful.

Seth's cell phone, dangling from a holster at his side, jarred the quiet lakeside and saved her from saying more.

Seth slapped at the device, yanking it to his mouth. "Washington."

He listened intently. A deep vee formed

between his eyebrows. "I'll check it out and let you know."

Seth ended the call and stood staring at the phone. "County dispatcher. We've had another break-in."

Kat straightened, all thoughts of her own worries disappearing like smoke in a gale. Wilson's Cove was her home. What happened here concerned her. "Where?"

"Bill Novotny's place out on Sand Creek Road."

"Bill! I saw him and Agnes at the bank earlier today. Are they okay?"

"Don't know. I hope so." He jogged up the incline toward his truck.

"Agnes has a heart condition," Kat called after him.

He spun around. "Want to go with me? She may need your help."

Kat hesitated for only a second. "Let me get my bag."

Chapter Seven

As he sped toward Sand Creek Road, Seth was glad to have Kat riding shotgun. The fact that she was a doctor and Agnes Novotny had heart trouble was one reason. He didn't like thinking about the other reason, but it was there. The more he was with Kathryn, the more he wanted to be.

He was an idiot.

"What's in the bag?" He nodded toward the black leather bag that looked surprisingly like the ones he'd seen in old-time movies. "I thought you didn't have any doctor stuff here?"

"Just some basic equipment and meds. One of my colleagues sent them down at my request."

"Really?" Now that was interesting. She was leaving medicine but wanted to have supplies on hand. Hmm.

She must have read his thoughts because she stiffened. "These are my personal items,

Seth. Having them sent here is no big deal."

Maybe not, but why would a woman who wanted to leave her profession have medical equipment mailed to her?

He lifted his fingers from the wheel. "Hey, I'm not complaining. This town needs all the help we can get."

The tension in her shoulders relaxed. "Sorry. I didn't mean to bite your head off."

He let her off the hook but was too smart not to realize that the subject of her career hit a nerve because she wasn't through being a doctor. She'd go back. He had no doubt. Maybe she just needed a little push in the right direction.

"These break-ins make everyone tense. This is the first one that's happened during the week."

"Is that significant?"

"I have no idea. Yet. Could be a copy cat or something different entirely."

Dust spewed out behind the wheels of his truck as he took a curve then slammed to a stop outside the Novotnys' big rambling farmhouse. Bill Novotny stepped off the front porch as Kat jumped out of the truck.

"Are you all right?" she called, hurrying across the neatly mowed yard. Yellow and red tulips nodded from tidy flower beds around the front porch.

"Mad as the dickens but not hurt. Whoever busted in was gone when we got home from town."

"What about Agnes?"

He jerked a thumb toward the house. "She's in the bedroom crying her heart out. Dirty buzzards broke some of the knickknacks she's saved since our kids was babies."

"Mind if I check on her?"

"I'd appreciate it."

Kat tapped at the door, hollered, "Agnes," and stepped inside the house.

If Bill thought there was anything strange about Kathryn Thatcher riding along with the lake ranger, he didn't say so.

"Come on in, Seth, I'll show you what they done."

Boots echoed as the men crossed the wooden porch and entered the house. The living room appeared unmolested, but when they entered the kitchen, Seth's heart sank to his heels. Broken dishes lay scattered in shards on the countertops and floor. Food, some of it half-eaten, had been dragged from the refrigerator and left lying about. This was the messiest scene yet.

"Appears they were looking for something," he said grimly, taking in the cabinets thrown wide. "Probably money or liquor.

Did you keep anything like that in here?"

His jowls sagging, Bill nodded. "Mama kept a Mason jar of old coins up on the top shelf. Mostly nickels and dimes and pennies, but some silver dollars, too. It's gone."

Seth surveyed the mess, snapping photos with a tiny pocket camera and making notes as he went. "Anything else you've noticed missing?"

"In the bedroom." The farmer motioned with his head. "My varmint gun. Agnes may have found other things missing by now. She was still looking."

Seth clenched his jaws. A gun stolen. He didn't like that at all. Teenagers on a wild spree was one thing. Stolen guns could turn deadly.

Disheartened and concerned, Seth moved through the house with caution, looking for any hint of who had done this. He needed to find them and find them fast before someone got hurt.

Inside the bedroom, Kat sat on the side of a four-poster next to Agnes. The older lady lay with a broken photo gripped against her chest and a wad of tissues pressed to her face. Kat, who looked startlingly professional with a stethoscope around her neck, had applied a blood pressure cuff to the woman's arm.

"I can't believe anyone would do this to us," Agnes sobbed. "We never hurt a soul that I know of."

"Now, Mama," Bill said, coming over to gently pat his wife's hair. His thick hand looked big and reddened against her gray hair. "We're all right. That's what matters. These are only material things. You and me have weathered greater storms than this. Remember what we always say? As long as we got each other and the Lord, we can whup anything."

Agnes looked up at her husband, red-eyes brimming with tears, and managed a watery smile. She pulled his weatherworn hand against her cheek and patted it. Drawing in a shuddering breath, she stifled the sobs though tears rolled onto her husband's hand. "I know it, honey. I know it. We'll be all right."

Seth got a lump in his throat watching the quiet love between the older couple. Truly, this was the way God intended for a man and a woman to live together for a lifetime.

His gaze strayed to Kat's face. She'd become intensely interested in the star pattern on the bedspread. He could tell she was feeling the emotion, too.

"You rest now, Mama," Bill said, "and do whatever Kathryn tells you to, all right? Me and Seth here will take care of everything else."

Seth cleared his throat. "Right. We sure will. Kat, will you look after Mrs. Novotny?"

Kat's blue eyes shifted to him. Moisture glistened in their depths. "Sure. Let me know if I can help in any other way."

With a jerky nod, Seth started through the rest of the house, searching for clues. Bill trailed along, making pithy comments about buzzards and weasels who would do such a thing. Seth had to concur.

The vandals had entered through a bathroom window. He swept the sill for fingerprints. Outside the window, he discovered several sets of footprints, mostly tennis shoes, he thought. The idea of a bunch of punks breaking into the homes of decent people had angered him as a city cop and it angered him even more here in this peaceful setting.

Jaw tight, blood pressure pounding in his temples, he stood in the fading sun and phoned a report to the county sheriff. Bill, carrying a tire iron, walked around the outbuildings and barn.

Back inside the house Seth found Kat sweeping up glass in the kitchen.

"Nice of you," he commented.

"I don't want Agnes worrying with this.

She's having some palpitations."

Alarm flared in him. The worst thing about living in a small town was this. In emergencies, help was too far away.

"Does she need an ambulance?"

"I don't think so. She's taken her meds, and I phoned her physician in Henderson to be on the safe side."

He would never have thought of that, but then he wasn't a doctor. If Agnes had so much as passed out or grabbed her chest, he would have been pretty much helpless without Kat. "I'm glad you came along."

She didn't answer and Seth got the message. She wanted to leave the career she'd sacrificed everything to gain, but the career didn't want to leave her.

Brown hair falling forward, she finished sweeping the glass into a pile. Seth found the dustpan and went down on one knee to hold it for her.

She smiled. "Thanks."

Interesting how that one word and a smile could make him feel so happy. Here he was in the middle of a troubling investigation and he was admiring Kat's smile.

This was not a good sign.

"I'm about finished with my report," he said. "I could help you clean up."

He knew the offer would make her smile

again. Wasn't that partly why he'd made it?

"Grab a trash bag, ranger, and start shoveling the smashed food into it. The garbage can is out the back door there." She pointed. "If you'll haul trash, I'll run a sponge mop over this mess."

"For a doctor, you know a lot about cleaning up after vandals."

"Agnes will want to clean things her way tomorrow when she's feeling better, I'm sure. But this will take some of the stress off tonight."

They worked companionably, and in no time the kitchen was presentable. As they finished, Bill rumbled in from outside carrying a galvanized bucket.

"The garden is making good." He clunked the silver bucket onto the now clean table. "Here's some fresh green beans and new potatoes for you. Stuck a couple of cabbage heads and a few green onions in there, too."

Seth accepted the gifts, knowing the farmer was showing his appreciation in the best way he knew.

"These are great, Bill. Thanks." Though he normally wasn't much of a cook, with Alicia visiting, he was trying to do better. Playing the single dad was harder than he'd expected.

127

At the thought of his daughter, Seth jerked.

Oh, man. He had promised to pick her up at four. He looked at his watch, though the fact that the sky blazed orange with the sunset told him the appointed time was long past.

With a groan, he yanked his cell phone from its holder and punched in numbers.

Some father he was.

"Stop beating yourself up, Seth. You're late because of your job, because you were helping someone in need."

Kat's words should have been a salve to his conscience, but Seth wasn't mollified. He'd let Alicia down. Letting women down seemed to be the story of his life.

"I should have remembered. I should have called her sooner."

"Didn't she say she was having fun and hadn't even noticed the time?"

Well, yes, she had said that. She'd also said Derek had just stopped in to watch a movie with her and Shelby. She'd actually sounded glad that he was late.

"I shouldn't have forgotten."

"You weren't exactly twiddling your thumbs all this time. These break-ins are bad business."

They were for certain. "I need to go back out there and talk to the neighbors, see if they noticed anything out of the ordinary."

"The closest neighbors are nearly a mile away."

"But a vehicle would have to drive down that road to get to the Novotny place. If they were in a vehicle."

"You think they may have walked in through the woods?"

"Possibly. Especially if the vandals are local." He'd check out the woods tomorrow, too.

"I'm just glad the Novotnys weren't at home. Who knows what might have happened."

"So far, only empty houses have been hit."

"Agnes was so upset. Bless her heart."

"You were great with her. You're a good doctor."

"Was."

"Come on, Kat. Be real. You can't throw away all those years of training and experience."

"Don't you think I'm capable of doing anything else?"

"Why would you want to? Being a doctor is all you ever wanted."

Remember? He longed to say. Remember how much more important a medical career was than anything else? Than him?

He remembered and the notion stuck in his craw like a dry cracker. He shouldn't care anymore, but he did.

"I'd like to buy a business here in Wilson's Cove."

"Why?"

She gave him an exasperated look. "Would you stop saying why?"

He couldn't resist. "Why?"

Kat laughed. "Because."

Seth chuckled and some of the tension building up in his brain seeped away. Kat had always been able to calm him down and make him smile, even when life had been lousy. And it had definitely been lousy back then. A man had to appreciate a woman like that.

"What kind of business do you have in mind?" he asked.

"The marina is for sale. Or I've thought about buying a fastfood franchise. Wilson's Cove could use more businesses."

"Good ideas, but the marina is seasonal."

"Not if I added something to it."

"Such as?"

"The fast-food franchise maybe or an arcade to attract teenagers. There is nothing for kids to do in the winter."

"True."

"Do you think I could do it?" A fretful pucker formed between her eyebrows. Was she actually worried that she couldn't?

"Make a go of a new business? No doubt in my mind. You're smart. You're not afraid of hard work. You'd do great."

But no matter what Kat said, Seth didn't believe for one minute she would stick around long enough to invest in a business or even to move back into her own cabin.

With a sinking heart, he realized one cold, hard fact. He'd like for Kat to stick around, but he knew she wouldn't.

The sooner Dr. Kat Thatcher recognized the truth about herself and went back to the career she loved, the better off he would be.

A germ of an idea took root.

Maybe, just maybe, he could help Kat make up her mind.

Kat sat at her sister's kitchen table, documents and brochures spread out around her in organized groups. A half-dozen kids of various ages wandered in and out, poking their heads into the refrigerator and then disappearing up the stairs or out the back door. Amidst the traffic, Susan brewed richly scented Italian coffee, dispensed cookies and sodas and listened to Kat's latest enterprise.

"My accountant says a food place would make the most money," Kat said, gnawing on the end of a yellow mechanical pencil.

Susan pushed the button on the blender and silenced all conversation to mix a coffee and flavoring concoction with ice and milk.

When the noise ceased, Kat shot her an amused look. "You don't think this is a good idea, do you?"

"What? You buying a business here in Wilson's Cove?"

"Isn't that what we've been talking about for the last half hour?"

Susan plunked a frothy glass in front of Kat. "Try that. You'll love it."

Kat sipped, but she wasn't letting the question go unanswered. "Yum. You're going to turn me into a flavored coffee freak if you keep making these. I'll go broke buying five-dollar cups of coffee."

"Not around here you won't. Besides, those fancy coffee places don't have anything on me. And I'm much cheaper. This is my special blend of espresso, strawberry syrup and sweetened condensed milk."

"With whipped cream on top, of course." Kat licked the sweet mustache from her upper lip. "Not a bit of fat or cholesterol."

"Of course not." With a grin, Susan dragged a chair to the table and rested her chin on her hands. "Do you really like it?"

"This stuff is amazing. Seriously. You could open a shop." Suddenly Kat sat upright. "That's a great idea, Suz. I can front the money and you can create the recipes and together we'll run the shop."

Susan's dark curls bounced as she shook her head. "I don't think so."

Kat studied her sister's expression. "You still don't think I'm serious, do you?"

"Truth? No. I think once the lawsuit is settled and you get over being tired and angry, you'll get in that little blue car and high-tail it back to Oklahoma City. And maybe, if we're lucky, you'll come home for Thanksgiving or Christmas."

Heaviness weighed in on Kat. No one wanted to listen to how she really felt. Even though she still struggled with emptiness and a lack of purpose, she was sure a new business enterprise would solve the problem.

"You're wrong," she said. "So please, for today, pretend to believe in me. I want your honest opinion on these business opportunities."

She bent her head to study a spreadsheet detailing the projected income for a fast-food franchise. According to the demographics info, the cove was ripe for meals that campers and fisherman could grab on the go. If she felt a little guilty as a physician to buy into a business that was the antithesis of good health, she kept it to herself.

"What does Seth say?" Susan asked, trying but failing to sound offhand.

Kat's head jerked up. "Seth has nothing to do with any of my plans."

Susan ran her fingers up and down the condensing glass. "I think he'd like to."

"And where do you get your information? At the Quick Mart?"

"Everyone in town has seen the two of you together a lot lately." Susan sipped her drink, watching Kat over the rim. "People talk."

"He's working on my dock."

"Interesting. There are plenty of other docks that need repair, as well as the ranger's house. And there's no reason for you to help him shop for supplies or stop off at Cherry's for a burger."

Kat sipped her own drink, savoring the cold mocha flavor, while she considered Susan's statement. What her sister said was true, she supposed, though she'd refused to credit Seth's frequent appearances and requests that she "ride along" into town. He'd asked her opinion on colors and decor, nothing personal or earth-shattering in that. But since the Novotny break-in, she'd seen him every single day.

At times she'd questioned her sanity, but when she was alone for too long, oppressive thoughts came to visit and stayed the night. Being with Seth seemed to help. He was good company, a nice guy with a wicked sense of humor and a solid sense of who he was and what he wanted. Unlike her.

He had matured into a steady, confident, unselfish man of faith, though he never pushed about his relationship with God. She was impressed. So much so, that she'd begun thinking about God again, but she didn't share that tidbit with Susan. Today was a day for researching her options, not for a lesson in finding God's will.

"Do you think Seth is interested in me? I mean, as a woman?" Kat asked softly, staring blindly into her coffee.

"What do *you* think?"

"Ah, Susan." Kat inhaled deeply and breathed out in a gust that wiggled the whipped cream. "I don't know. I don't think anything good could come of it. Seth and I hurt each other so much back then."

"You're different people now."

Yes, but growing older didn't change what they'd done.

"I like him. He's a terrific guy." A guy who could hurt her. "I don't think his daughter likes me much though."

"Alicia?" Susan pushed her frothy coffee to one side. "What makes you say that?"

Kat shrugged. "Most times she's polite enough, but sometimes she gives me these suspicious looks as if she wished I'd go away."

"Maybe she's jealous because she suspects her dad is interested in you."

"He said she harbors the fantasy that he and her mother will get back together."

"Poor kid. It's a common fantasy for kids of divorced parents, but painful just the same."

"Seth tends to give in to her too much, I think."

"Another problem of divorce. The non-custodial parent feels guilty, whether warranted or not, and spoils his child because he feels she's been hurt enough already. Divorce is an ugly mess, no way around it."

"How do you know so much about children of divorce?" Kat asked, amused, as she took another sip of the creamy concoction.

Susan threw her hands into the air. "Dr. Phil. Where else?"

Sputtering with laughter, Kat swallowed a lump of ice. She fanned her face and coughed until Susan leaped up, also laughing and pounded her back.

Kat was too choked up to explain that pounding the back was not in the least bit useful.

When the fit subsided, tears ran down Kat's face but she continued to grin. "Could we please get back to these papers? I've narrowed my decision to three. Help me decide."

"I'm not going to let you duck the questions about Seth."

"I don't have any answers, Susan. I don't know."

"How do you feel about him?"

"Don't ask me that. I don't know."

"When was the last time you dated anyone on a regular basis?"

Longer than she wanted to admit. "My career keeps me busy."

"Your career has stolen your life."

The blunt statement shocked Kat and yet, hadn't she recently complained that she had no life outside of the hospital? "I don't even know if I want a life."

"Then why are you here?" Susan reached across the table and put her hand over Kat's. In a soft voice, she said, "I love you.

For years I've prayed for you to find fulfillment and joy in your life. I'd hoped you had, but deep inside I knew better. You're an incredible physician. You're also a wonderful, caring, attractive woman. You deserve a life."

"Not everyone wants your kind of life, Susan."

Her sister sat back. "Maybe not. But you're searching for something. At least admit that much."

Kat tilted her head in acquiescence. Something *was* wrong in her life, but she hadn't figured out what it was. She'd thought by immersing herself in medicine she would be fulfilled. Yet all the while, some nagging need had lingered in the back of her heart. Then she'd hit professional burnout and walked away with nothing. No career. No personal life. Nothing.

"The Lord hasn't forgotten about you, sis."

Susan's words pressed a sore place like someone poking a bruise, because the truth was, Kat *had* felt forsaken by God.

When Kat remained silent, Susan, the gentle bulldog, went on. "Seth Washington hasn't forgotten you, either. He's such a great guy and by all appearances, he is here to stay. If you're really serious about remaining in Wilson's Cove, why not go with the flow and see what happens?"

Kat bent her head to the paperwork at hand, but her mind was on Seth. Susan was right. He was a fine man and he did continue to seek her out, whatever his motives. He'd also told her more than once that he'd found what he was looking for here in the cove and would never leave again. This was the life for him.

The question was: Was this the life for her? Was she doing the right thing?

Part of her cried yes, but another part was scared and depressed.

She studied the papers some more, fretting. Could she make a go of a totally foreign business enterprise? What if she failed? What then?

The house phone rang. Kat glanced up as Susan answered on the second ring. Wearing her best "I told you so" look, her sister handed the phone to Kat. "Seth needs your help."

"Seth?" Kat said into the receiver. "Is everything all right?"

"Nothing serious. I ran into a fisherman with a hook in his hand. I was wondering if you could help him out."

Oh. "Single or three-way?"

"Three-way."

"Where are you?"

"I can be at your place in five minutes."

"Okay." She started to ring off and then asked, "How did you know I was here?"

"Alicia told me."

"That makes sense." Alicia had been here earlier but left with Derek. Kat wondered if Seth knew that. Before she could ask, he said, "Why don't you have your cell phone turned on?"

Kat glanced around the kitchen but didn't see her purse. "I must have left it in the car."

"Left the car unlocked too, didn't you?" She caught the disapproval in his gravelly tone.

"Bye, Seth. See you in five." She returned the phone to Susan and stood to leave. "Someone has a fish hook in his hand."

"Don't sound so annoyed. The poor fisherman is the one in pain."

"I'm not practicing medicine anymore. Why can't anyone get the message?"

"You could have refused."

One hand on the doorknob, Kat paused. She hadn't even considered refusing.

Now why, she wondered, was that?

CHAPTER EIGHT

The incident with the fisherman was the first of several such minor medical "emergencies" to appear at Kathryn's door over the next weeks. If she had a suspicious nature — and she did — Kat would suspect someone was up to something.

A misty rain hissed against the warm concrete as she finished filling her gas tank and went inside the Quick Mart to pay and grab a cup of coffee. Any kind of rain was welcome in an Oklahoma summer. She was greeted by the town's unofficial news reporter, Donna Parks.

The large-boned woman stood behind the counter, smiling warmly. "Kat, honey. How ya doin'?"

Kat smiled back. Even if Donna loved to gather and disseminate gossip, she was kindhearted and friendly.

"I'm doing pretty well. Yourself?"

"Fit as a fiddle." The computer register

chinged as she took Kat's money. "Bill No-votny was in here this morning bragging on you."

"How are he and Agnes doing since the break-in?"

"Better, I think." Donna slapped fists on her hips. "It just burns my biscuits to think someone would break in on a nice old couple like that."

"Mine, too. Any rumors as to the guilty party?"

"A few of the kids that come in here are acting funny lately. Could be nothing at all and if they know anything, no one is spilling the beans. I told Seth. He's a good man, checking on everything. The town was sure lucky to get him." She pushed a plastic coffee lid toward Kat. "Seeing you two together again is like old times. How you getting along with that little girl of his?"

Fighting back the urge to explain yet again that she and Seth were not a couple, she simply said, "Alicia's all right. Still adjusting to a small town."

Donna chuckled. "I noticed she was kind of citified. She comes in here sometimes with that Grimes boy to play video games." She snapped her fingers. "Oh, listen, I just remembered. Matty Seaforth passed yesterday afternoon. The funeral's set for day after

142

tomorrow at the church. Ten o'clock."

Kat had no idea how Donna had made the segue from video games to an elderly resident's death, but that was Donna.

"I'm sorry to hear that." She didn't know the Seaforths well. They'd retired on the lake after she'd gone away to college, but they attended Susan's church. "Susan will want to know."

"And Seth, too. Make sure you tell him." Kat nodded. No use pointing out that Donna could tell Seth just as easily. "The dinner is in the fellowship hall after the service. I hope Susan will bring that sweet potato casserole again. She made it for the last funeral." Donna tapped her cheek. "Let's see, who was that? Jack Sherril? Anyway, I've thought of that casserole a hundred times."

"I'll tell her," Kat said, hiding a smile as she edged toward the door. "Thanks, Donna. I need to run now."

"Lands, yes, you must have people lined up waiting to see you."

Kat paused, one hand on the glass door. "Pardon?"

"The whole town is tickled pink that you're opening an office here. We've needed a doctor for a long time, and who better than someone we all know and trust. Why,

143

you can't beat a deal like that with a sledge-hammer."

Kat blinked. The rumors about her and Seth weren't a surprise, but this was one. "I'm not opening an office in Wilson's Cove."

"You're not? Well, we just figured you were." Donna looked as bewildered as Kat felt. "I mean, you've been looking at buildings and businesses for days now. Everybody thought . . ."

Oh. The jump to conclusions was a logical leap.

"For investing," she said simply, not caring to explain further, lest the gossip become even more convoluted. "Not to open a medical practice."

"Well, that's a crying shame." The crest-fallen woman shook her head from side to side. "Wait till I tell Sharon."

Kat had no doubt she would do exactly that. To avoid providing more fodder for the grapevine, Kat waved goodbye and pushed open the door, spoke to the man entering and stepped outside. A hand-lettered sign announcing the cheerleader carwash was stuck to the front window with Scotch tape. Below that, someone had posted a photo of a litter of pups looking for a new home.

Kat smiled. The photo reminded her of

144

Sadie's mama cat, the one Sadie carried around like a baby, complete with little clothes and bonnet. Queenie was due to have kittens soon. Perhaps Kat should adopt one. A pet would be good company and help convince everyone that she was here to stay, including herself.

But not for the purpose of opening a medical practice.

The rain had stopped, leaving the concrete shiny and dark and the air smelling clean and fresh. Kat sipped at her rapidly cooling coffee and tried to process the whirlwind of information gathered in the short visit.

The very idea that she might consider setting up a practice here would send her accountant into cardiac arrest. No doctor could make a living in such a tiny town.

She slammed her car door and cranked the engine.

It was not even a possibility.

"Why not give the idea some consideration? The cove needs a doctor." Seth sat in a metal folding chair, arms across his chest, booted feet propped on the bottom rung of a stepladder, his back aching from unloading six full boxes of floor tile.

Kat had appeared at the rangers' house where he was working, bringing along

Susan's meat loaf dinner and pecan bars and the news that one of the cove's residents had passed away. He'd been a little surprised to have Kat seek him out, but he couldn't deny the leap of happiness when he'd seen her exit the Toyota.

Now she leaned against his kitchen counter relating the misguided gossip that she intended to open a medical office in the cove. The gossip disturbed her, and Seth thought she looked pretty cute standing there, all worked up, trying to rationalize away a decent idea.

"The cost of setting up a practice in a small town is off-putting," she said. "Most physicians stay clear, opting for cities or larger towns with medical centers. Business is slow in a small place, and by the time I hired someone to battle the insurance companies and pay the overhead, I'd be working for nothing."

"You sound as if you've thought about it."

"Not really." A five-gallon bucket of paint and a pile of tools and supplies sat against one stripped wall. She scooted the bucket around and perched on the top. "But doctors discuss these things. Lots of us would enjoy living in a small town, but after the years and expense of medical school and residency, small-town practices are not cost effective."

"It was just an idea."

"Which wouldn't work for me, Seth."

"I hear you." But he was disappointed. If she was really interested in sticking around town, it made sense to him that she would do what she loved most — practice medicine. The fact that she was adamantly opposed to the idea was pretty telling, in his opinion. Argue all she wanted, she wasn't committed to living here.

Wilson's Cove needed a doctor badly. The distance from the lake to Henderson was too far to be worth the trip for small things as well as being too far for safety in a real emergency. The firemen in the area served as first responders, but they were all volunteers with minimal training and equipment.

He uncrossed his arms and twisted from side to side, hoping to relieve the catch in his back. "Don't you miss the work?"

"A little."

"Maybe you should go on back to the City sooner instead of later."

Her smile was easy. She pulled her knees up and hugged them, chin resting on her folded arms. Brown hair tumbled over one shoulder. "Trying to get rid of me?"

The question was loaded and too complicated to answer without more explanation than Seth was prepared to give. Kathryn Thatcher had handed him his heart on a platter once before, and a wise man didn't let that happen twice. But he couldn't deny he felt something for her as a man.

He also felt something as a Christian, a responsibility for her discarded faith. Lately, she'd stopped bristling whenever he talked about his relationship to Jesus and that gave him hope. He wanted to do the right thing, both for himself and her. He just didn't know for certain what that was.

As he twisted again, a muscle spasm grabbed him. With a groan, he rotated forward to relieve the pressure.

Kat dropped her feet to the floor and came to attention. "What's wrong?"

He offered a smile, which was more a grimace considering the stab of pain. "You wouldn't know a fancy medical trick for curing back spasms, would you?"

Frowning, she looked him over, her tone both exasperated and concerned. "What did you do to yourself? Let me have a look."

She crossed to where he sat and crouched in front of him. Though he'd seen it before, the rapid transformation from friend to concerned professional amazed him. One minute she was Kat, the woman, worrying over what to do with her life, and the next she was Dr. Thatcher, competent, concerned and confident.

Fool that he was he liked them both.

He told her about lifting the tile. "Muscle strain maybe?"

"Probably," she mused, eyes narrowed in concentration. "Describe the pain. Show me where you hurt."

He did.

"Stand up. Let me check some things."

Professional hands roamed over his back, pressing, rotating his arms and neck, instructing him to move in certain ways, asking questions that told him she knew exactly what she was doing.

He couldn't help it if he enjoyed having her touch him, even in an objective manner.

Yes, he could be in trouble if he wasn't careful.

When she completed her exam, she said, "I'm confident you have either a muscle or a lumbar strain. Either way, the treatment is the same. Anti-inflammatory and rest. I can write a prescription for muscle relaxers if you need them." She searched his face, well-trained eyes gauging the tension in his expression. "And you probably do. You aren't a whiner."

No, he wasn't. He normally pushed through the pain of about anything and kept working. In more than ten years on the force, he'd taken all of two sick days, one when Alicia was born and another when he'd been shot in the foot and the chief had insisted. "Muscle relaxers? Will they interfere with my job?"

"You can't drive or operate machinery while taking them."

"Nope. No pills then." This time of year when the summer people arrived, he was super busy around the lake. Add to that the vandalism and remodeling this house, and he had no time to nurse a sore back.

"In that case, over-the-counter ibuprofen may be your best option. If it doesn't work, let me know and we'll reassess. For sure, no lifting for a couple of weeks until this resolves."

Who was she kidding? "Too much work to do. Here at this house. At your place. Another rotten dock at cabin seven. The facilities on the north side of the lake need repair. I have camp sites to assess, trails to clear, and the list goes on and on. I can't stop everything for two weeks."

"Well then, stubborn, your back may not get better for a while."

"The price I have to pay, I guess." He took his ball cap from the counter and slapped it against his thigh. Dust motes danced in the air. "I've never had muscle spasms in my life. We're getting old, Kat."

"Speak for yourself, Washington."

"Seriously. Think about it. The Bible says our lives are like a passing shadow and sometimes I feel as if the shadow is passing at warp speed. We don't have a lot of time on this earth to do things right." Seth wasn't sure where he was going with this or why the idea had suddenly erupted in his brain.

Kat's serious blue gaze met his. "I've been thinking about that some, too. About the Bible, I mean, and God."

Seth sent a prayer of thanks winging toward heaven. He didn't want to push, but he wanted to be available. The fine line was tricky sometimes. "Anything I can do?"

She smiled and moved to the counter to fiddle with the still-warm food. "Keep praying for me. It's working."

Heart racing, he returned the smile. "You got it. And anything else you need."

There was the crux of the matter. If he admitted the truth, he needed Kat to need him. He needed to take five steps, pull her into his arms and promise to solve all her problems. He couldn't, of course. Only Kat and the Lord could work out the issues in her life. All he could do was keep praying and offer to be there, at least for the time being, another issue he couldn't resolve. Everything with Kathryn was temporary. He knew it whether she did or not. As a result, the time he spent with her was both pleasure and pain.

"You need some help around here," she said, smoothly changing the subject. Seth was glad. His head was doing crazy things again and a subject change was a great distracter. "Extra help would take some of the load off you — and your back."

"The town can't afford another full-time employee. They hired a couple of boys through a summer jobs program that help me out a lot. And we have the volunteer group that keeps the grounds clean. I don't know what I'd do without them. But other than that, the jobs are all mine."

"Couldn't the boys come here to the house and out on the docks to unload the heavy items? Or would that injure your masculine pride?"

"You're making me feel really old, but I suppose you're right. I keep them busy already, but they're good kids. They'll do whatever I ask."

He sneaked a peak under one of the foil covers. A delicious aroma wafted out. Kat patted his hand and laughed when he jerked away like a scolded kid.

"*I* could help," she said. "I've been meaning to do more on the dock but got side-
tracked. And I could help you here with the
ranger's house."

"No way." Kat here underfoot day in and
day out?

They stood face-to-face, each leaning
against the edge of the counter. Kat dipped
her head, a faint flush spreading over her
cheekbones.

"Okay, I understand. I just thought since
I helped you choose the outside paint —"
She waved one hand as if to erase the idea.
"Never mind. I'm terrible at that sort of
thing. I wouldn't be any help."

"Hey." He pulled her hand into his. "You
aren't terrible at anything, Kat. That wasn't
why I rejected the idea. But someone with
your education and training shouldn't be
stuck painting my living room."

Her eyes flicked up to his and down again.
"What if I wanted to?"

Oh, man.

Seth swallowed, acutely aware of Kat's
nearness and of her soft skin against his
work-roughened hand.

No matter how many years and experi-
ences separated them, Seth couldn't deny
he was feeling something special for Kat
Thatcher all over again. A smarter man

would get out while he could.

Too bad he'd never been that smart.

He forced a light tone. "Then I'd have to buy you a paint brush and invite you over."

Kat reached for his other hand, lacing her fingers with his. When she did things like that, his inner pep talks had little effect. Now only inches apart, Seth wondered if she could hear his heart pounding.

"Invite me," she said. "And I'll bring my own brush. Roller too."

"Consider yourself invited," he murmured, trying not to stare at her lips but failing. He'd kissed Kat, the teenage girl. What would it be like to kiss Kat, the woman?

"Will you teach me some more about carpentry, too?" those lips asked.

Seth blinked, shaking off his wayward thoughts. He really had some praying to do tonight. "You're serious?"

"I am. A woman alone should know how to do these things."

The words were a subtle reminder that she intended to remain alone. Okay. He would deal with that. He disengaged their hands and stepped back.

"I'll teach you anything you want to know."

"Good. When do we start?"

"Your call." Hadn't it always been?

"Here's my idea." She pointed at him. "You sit back down in this chair, feet elevated, and take some ibuprofen. I'll dish up Susan's meat loaf and we'll formulate a plan."

Seth managed a wry grin. "Always the type-A personality. Gotta have a plan."

"Yeah," she said softly as she slid a hefty slice of meat loaf onto a plate. "That's me. Planning and scheming and going nowhere." She slanted a look at him and gave a little laugh. "I've been thinking about what you said the other day."

"Which was?"

"The thing in the Bible about God having a plan for our lives that was better than anything we can come up with on our own. Do you really believe that?"

She was serious. Seth's pulse leaped with hope.

"I won't deny that I've questioned God a few times, but He's been my comfort and strength even through those times."

Holding on to the top of the chair, he eased to the seat and gingerly propped his boots on the ladder. The movement sent a twinge across the center of his back.

"That's my problem with God," she said, a pretty frown forming between her golden eyebrows as she plopped roasted potatoes and zucchini next to the meat loaf. "If He has good plans for us, why did your wife divorce you?"

Seth had wrestled this same question for many months. Finally peace had come. Not an outright answer, but peace. It would have to do.

"I'm not sure, Kat. I wish I had all the answers, but I don't. Maybe the plan is bigger than a divorce or sickness, bigger than anything we perceive as bad. Maybe we have to live life, taking God at his word, living as close to his will as we can, and someday when we look back at the big picture, we'll see how perfectly His plan unfolded. Because the truth is, we can make all the plans we want to, but there are going to be some things we can't ever control. Maybe we aren't supposed to. Maybe that's where trusting God comes into play."

Behind the blue eyes, Kat's bright mind was processing. Seth remained quiet and let her think. Truth was, he didn't know what else to say.

After a bit, she handed him the plate and said, "That's really deep and philosophical, Seth."

"Nah. Just the ramblings of a man who's been lifted out of some pretty dark places by God's grace. I'm no answer man, but it is something to think on."

"Indeed."

Seth picked up his fork and began to eat the hearty meal, figuring he'd said enough for now. In Kat's life, she'd tried to plan and control everything. A few times he'd done the same. Had all their efforts made them happy? He didn't think so.

Kathryn spooned helpings of Susan's meat loaf and veggies onto a plate for herself, the spicy scent of pepper and onion comforting in a Southern kind of way.

If someone would have told her a few months ago that she would be propped on a paint can as comfortable as could be talking with Seth Washington about life and religion, she would have laughed them to shame. But she was. Between Susan's pointed questions and the town's assumption that she and Seth were together, she should be running in the other direction.

Perhaps the reason she hadn't was Seth himself. He made her feel safe. At the same time, he'd urged her to leave town, to go back to her life in Oklahoma City. But he'd also suggested she open a medical practice here. In other words, Seth was supporting her decision whatever that might be. Not one other person had been as generous.

She wondered what Seth was really thinking and feeling, but didn't ask. One thing for certain, he didn't hate her. She'd thought he might. Fear of his contempt was one of the reasons she'd avoided seeing him again for so long. He had a right to despise her, but Seth Washington had never had it in him to hate anyone. And he'd improved with age. Kat feared she hadn't.

She sighed, louder than intended.

Seth cocked his head. "You're thinking heavy thoughts."

"Yes, I am."

"Want to talk about them?"

She shook her head. "Not now."

Though he studied her face for several long, searching seconds, he didn't press. She was grateful. She needed to work things out on her own. But wasn't it lovely knowing he would listen without judgment?

Returning to her bucket seat, she balanced the plate on her lap. "Where's Alicia this afternoon? I haven't seen her at Susan's in the last couple of days."

Seth scooped a bite of potatoes onto his fork. "She and Derek stopped in to raid my tackle box right after lunch. They're boat fishing near here."

"I thought she hated fishing." She grinned,

CHAPTER NINE

Seth reacted so fast Kat could hardly believe he'd been having muscle spasms a few minutes ago. He burst out the door and into the sunlight, sore back forgotten in the adrenaline rush to get to his child. As Kat followed, running behind him in the direction of the latest screams, she caught the flash of sunlight on his pistol and the distinct ratchet as the metal clip locked and loaded.

At another scream, the hair stood up on the back of her neck. Seth gathered speed, his boots thudding against hard ground.

Just out of the yard a series of narrow trails led into the woods or down to the lake at various points. Seth paused in the dappled sunlight to listen. Though his heart had to be thundering, he was quiet as death, not even breathing hard.

From somewhere ahead, a fierce growl erupted. Kat's first thought was "bear," but then another deep, spine-chilling growl was followed by a volley of wild, ferocious barks.

"Daddyyyy!" Alicia's quivering scream came again.

Seth moved then, bolting down a trail toward the sound, dodging limbs and taking hits from others. Kat followed a safe distance behind, unsure what they might encounter but wanting to be there if Alicia was injured.

As Seth rounded a bend, he suddenly stopped dead still. Behind him Kat froze. At the sight ahead, fear rose in her throat like a virus.

A broad-bodied pit bull stood in the trail, lips curled, long fangs bared, slobbering with every staccato bark. He must have weighed in at a hundred pounds and the power in his front legs and jowls would strike terror in any sensible human. Every hair on his body stood up, quivering with ferocity. He lunged over and over toward something just off the trail.

Fear snaked up Kat's spine. The dog must be focused on Alicia.

Seth raised his firearm. Though he had to be winded and hurting, his aim was steady and sure. Kat had no doubt Seth would do whatever had to be done to protect his daughter . . . and her.

"Don't move," he said quietly, slowly dropped one hand to his side to motion her back. "Stay behind me. If he attacks I'll take him down." Without raising his voice, he said, "Alicia, where are you?"

Somehow over the deafening snarls and barks, they heard Alicia's quivering reply "Up here, Daddy."

Seth never took his eyes off the vicious dog.

"Can you see her?" he murmured to Kat.

Kat slowly, slowly looked up and spotted the terrified girl. She was visibly trembling, her eyes wide with terror.

Whispering, Kat said, "She's in the tree about four feet above the dog."

The muscular animal surged forward then, toward Seth, a warning to back off. Heart pounding erratically, Kat jumped, afraid the dog would attack any minute. Seth held his ground.

"Is she hurt?" His tone remained as calm as if they were discussing a fishing trip.

Kat made eye contact with Alicia, questioning. The teary girl shook her head.

"I don't think so. Just very scared."

Some of the tension seeped out of Seth's shoulders.

"Thank God." He aimed the pistol above and to the right of the animal, opposite

Alicia's safe haven. "Hold your ears."

The shot exploded, echoing back a thousand times. Even covered, Kat's ears rang from the blast. The dog, though unstruck, seemed shocked into silence but didn't leave. Seth fired again, this time closer. The animal yelped and scurried away into the underbrush.

Seth lowered the pistol and whirled toward his daughter. "Alicia, baby, are you all right?"

She nodded, sobs shuddering through her. "I . . . I think so."

"Come down. He's gone." He stuffed the weapon into his back waistband and lifted his hands toward her. "Come on. Daddy's got you. You're safe now."

The sweetness in Seth's words touched Kat's heart. The big, tough cop had to be in pain, but as his daughter slithered backward down the tree trunk, he swung her into his arms.

Alicia buried her face in her father's shoulder and sobbed. Her whole body trembled with the knowledge of what might have occurred. "Daddy, I was so scared. I thought he was going to kill me."

Kat had treated enough dog maulings to know such tragedies happened. Handled incorrectly, a pit bull was a dangerous animal.

Seth's hands and eyes raced over Alicia. "Did he bite you?"

"No." She sniffed and shuddered, then lifted one heel for inspection. "He grazed my ankle when I climbed the tree, but I think I'm okay."

"Kat will look at it." He lifted an eyebrow at Kat in silent question.

Till this point Kat had stood out of the way while Seth calmed his daughter, one eye on the woods where the dog had disappeared, her insides shaking from the close encounter. Now she moved closer and touched Alicia's shoulder.

"Let's go back to the house. I'll clean your ankle and make sure the skin wasn't broken. Okay?"

Alicia nodded. "My knees are shaking."

Kat could relate.

"Want to ride piggy back like you used to?" Seth asked. He offered a reassuring smile, though Kat saw the fear still lurking there.

With back spasms he shouldn't even be asking such a question.

"Dad, I'm not a baby."

The smile turned tender, squeezing Kat's heart. "You'll always be my baby, baby."

"I'm okay. Really." Though she trembled and was as white as the summer clouds, Alicia cast a final worried look behind her, and started down the trail. "Please don't let him come back and hurt me."

Jaw set, Seth brought up the rear. "Not a chance, baby. Not a chance."

When they reached the house, Alicia collapsed on the sheet-covered sofa, arms hugging her stomach. Kat brought her a glass of ice water. The girl had been through a trauma and, though unscathed physically, the experience wouldn't go away quickly.

"Here, honey, drink this."

Alicia shook her head. "I'm okay," she said again.

Face tear-stained and eyes reddened, she looked anything but okay. "An experience like that would shake anyone. You were incredibly smart to think of climbing a tree."

Alicia relented and took the glass from Kat's hand. "I didn't know what to do. I was hoping Daddy would hear me or I would get to the house, but the dog got closer and louder. Going up the tree was the only way I could think of to escape."

"Let me see your leg." Kat crouched in front of Alicia and examined the area on the back of her calf, pleased to encounter no signs of broken skin. "All I see is a red place on your ankle."

The girl shuddered. "He caught my ankle bracelet in his teeth and ripped it off. That's when I climbed the tree. I knew I couldn't run fast enough."

Seth, who had been pacing the floor, a scowl on his face, spun toward his daughter. "Where's Derek? You were supposed to be with him? Why wasn't he with you?"

Kat could read the protective male wheels turning in Seth's head. He had entrusted Alicia to another male's protection and Derek had let them both down.

Alicia must have sensed the ferocity in her father because she set the water glass aside and leaned forward to explain. "The fish weren't biting and Derek had some other stuff to do. I wanted to go home, so he took me to our cabin. He left, and after a while I got bored and decided to walk over here."

Seth's clenched fist opened. His shoulders relaxed. "Oh."

He stalked across the living room floor, around cans and boxes and paint rags, to perch on the edge of the couch beside his daughter. "Where were you when the dog first appeared?"

She described the area. "I walk through there all the time." So did Kat. "I've never seen him before."

"If he's wild or sick or even someone's watch dog that's gotten loose," Kat said, "he could be a real danger here on the lake where so many people are out in the open."

Seth's nostrils flared. "You're right about that. If you'll look after Alicia, I'll take the truck and search for him. I have a feeling I know where he came from."

"Where?" Wilson's Cove had never had leash laws, but maybe the time had come.

"A family bought the old Robertson farm a few months ago. Name of Shackley. Real unfriendly folks, chain-link fence, a passel of dogs, Keep Out signs all over the place. Suspicious bunch that I'm keeping an eye on. They have at least one pit bull running loose in the yard."

"Why didn't you shoot the dog?"

He scraped a hand over his face. "I sure wanted to. Maybe I should have, but I hate to shoot a man's dog without giving him a chance to take care of the problem first. Doesn't seem fair to the man or the dog."

"But we can't have any more incidents like this one. Too many children play around the lake in summer to have a vicious dog running loose."

"Couldn't agree more." He slapped the baseball cap onto his head. "Will you two be okay here for a while?"

Alicia cast Kat a look. "I want to go with you, Daddy."

Seth shook his head. "Not a good idea. I'm going to Shackleys' on official business."

"Then take me home. I don't want to stay *here*."

Kat heard the message loud and clear. She didn't want to be stuck here with Kat.

When Seth looked at her, a little embarrassed and at a loss, Kat said, "I really need to go, anyway. I have some business to take care of before five."

Yes, it was a lie, but she didn't know what else to do.

Seth looked relieved. "All right, then. Let's lock the place up and get moving."

The pit bull incident made the rounds of Wilson's Cove. For a few days Alicia and Seth were big news, although a lot of folks questioned Seth's decision not to kill the dog.

Kat, who loved to walk around the lake, had to admit she wasn't as comfortable now as she had been before. Hopefully, the Shackleys would keep their dogs better penned from now on. They claimed the animal was a guard dog who had never gotten loose before or caused a problem.

Kat hoped he never got loose again.

"Nobody much likes that Shackley bunch, anyway," Todd Berkett, owner of the marina, was saying to Kat. She'd stopped in at the marina to reserve a couple of rental jet skis for tomorrow afternoon with the nieces and nephew. "We all wish their kind wouldn't move to the Cove."

Kat had heard the sentiment repeated all over town. Susan would say they needed the Lord, but that was her answer to everyone's problems.

"Other than the dog situation, I don't think they've bothered anyone, have they?"

Todd shrugged. He was a huge man at over six and a half feet, with the weight to go with it. Sporting a full, shaggy beard complete with a yellow pencil stuck through it and overly long hair, he could easily have been mistaken for a member of some motorcycle gang. Newcomers were generally put off by Todd. Cove residents knew he was a teddy bear.

"Some folks are thinking they could be responsible for the break-ins. The trouble started not long after they moved here."

"I hadn't heard that. Does Seth know?"

"Not much gets by Seth. He knows. But he's not one to jump to conclusions."

Kat agreed. Seth was careful and thought

things out in a methodical, analytical manner. He would never make an accusation without hard evidence. But he would be watching. She was sure of that much.

"So," she said. "Can you hold those two machines for me?"

"Sure. Sure. Consider it done." He slid the pencil out of his beard, scribbled a note on a sticky pad, ripped it off and stuck the paper onto the desktop next to a dozen others. "You any closer to making a decision about buying this place?"

"Sorry, Todd, I'm not. I'll let you know as soon as I can." She felt badly about putting everyone off for so long, but the old restless uncertainty plagued her like mosquitoes. She simply did not know what she wanted to do. The more she investigated possibilities, the more depressed and unsure she became.

"I'm in no hurry, anyway. The more I think about it, the more I wonder how I'll feel to give up the place."

"Your family has owned the marina for a long time."

"That we have." He stuck the pencil back in his beard. With anyone but Todd, Kat would have considered the action weird. "You coming out to help with the kids' fishing tournament next weekend?"

"I hadn't thought about it. Why? Do I need to for some reason?"

"Oh, I just figured — I mean, Seth is the head honcho. I figured you'd know about it."

"No. I didn't." Kat's smile was tight as she turned to leave. Assumptions were starting to annoy her. Or maybe the fact that Seth hadn't mentioned the tournament annoyed her. She wasn't sure which. "See you later, Todd."

"Bye now, Kat. I mean, Dr. Thatcher."

"Kat," she corrected.

Stepping out into the sunshine, she drew in the sweet, clean smell of fresh air and started walking toward her cottage. One of the perks of lake living was the constant exercise along a beautiful route. Thought could flow easily in such a pristine environment, and if she lost a pound or two in the process, all the better.

Today she ruminated over the conversation with Todd; rumors that the Shackley family might be responsible for the break-ins; rumors about her and Seth that she wasn't ready to deal with; and the knowledge that Todd didn't really want to sell the marina.

There went her mind again, running in circles and going nowhere.

She picked up an empty snail shell and tossed it back and forth in her hands.

The lake was beautiful, matched only by the perfect weather. The water glistened gray blue, and only the smallest ripples disturbed the surface. Occasionally a fish flopped up in a somersault. Overhead huge fluffy clouds pillowed a sky so blue, her throat ached to look at such beauty.

She loved this place. Somewhere in all the confusion she'd forgotten how much.

Crossing the grounds of the marina, she headed around the curving beach area. When she and Susan were kids they'd played all along this shoreline and in the surrounding woods and hills, exploring caves and finding childish treasures like the snail shell in her hand. Their parents had never worried and the girls had never been afraid. She'd grown up in a safe and peaceful town, unaware of how rare such a place was. Sad to say, she thought the world had finally come to Wilson's Cove and brought its trouble along.

But as memories of yesteryear rolled over her, Kat felt nostalgic. She could almost hear Susan's laughter, almost see her father yanking the pull rope on the boat engine to take them fishing.

A lump rose in her throat. Not all her

memories were bad.

She needed to remember that.

The smallest breeze danced in from the lake and tickled her skin. She lifted her face in thanks and kept walking. The shoreline was rocky in places, grassy in some and sandy in yet others.

Boaters, bank fisherman and swimmers dotted the popular sandy area around the marina, but farther along, the shore grew more secluded and private. These were the areas the locals frequented.

Nearing one such area, Kat noticed a group of teenage boys riding jet skis just off the shore. Their laughter echoed over the water and made her smile.

Though still a hundred yards away, she could see their belongings scattered along the beach. A red-and-white ice chest, towels and shirts, a few crushed and discarded drink cans glinting in the sunlight. Boys traveled light.

By the time she neared the spot, one of the jet skis had come ashore. Two boys tumbled off the machine and began straightening the campsite. Their voices rose on the wind but the words were indistinct from this distance. Kat squinted against the sun, thinking she recognized the tall, athletic boy as Derek Grimes, Alicia's boyfriend.

"Dr. Thatcher, hey. How ya doin'?"

Yes, it was Derek, all right.

She smiled. "Looks like you boys are having a good time."

"Yes, ma'am. Sure are," Derek said.

The other boy snickered. "Real good."

Derek shot him a dirty look. "Shut up, Clint."

By now Kat was close enough to see the boys' faces. Both of them were flushed and their eyes were red. No big deal there. They were on the water and in the sun. But both of them appeared nervous, their gazes shifting away from hers. Something about their behavior didn't feel right.

"Is everything all right here, Derek?" she asked.

"Yeah. Why wouldn't it be?" His tone edged toward defensive. "We're just riding the jet skis and having a good time. Nothing wrong with that, is there?"

She wondered. "None at all. You boys have fun and be safe out there."

Clint sniggered again, and Kat speared him with a stare. He wouldn't meet her eyes. Suspicions edged into her consciousness as she recalled how quickly they'd come ashore and cleaned up their camp. Now she wondered why. What had they been doing that they hadn't wanted her see?

Drinking beer? Smoking pot?

Her heart sank. She hoped not. She didn't know Clint, but Derek went to Seth's church. He was considered a good kid. His family would be devastated, not to mention the danger he could be in. And Alicia didn't need to be dating a boy who used alcohol or drugs.

"Bye, Dr. Thatcher," Derek said, and whirled away from her searching gaze. As he reached the jet ski, he stumbled the slightest bit but kept upright and didn't look back. "Come on, Clint. The guys are waiting."

The jet ski roared to life and spun out across the serene lake leaving Kat to wonder. Should she mention the episode to anyone? To Susan? To Seth? Or should she mind her own business.

All the way back to her cabin she argued with herself. Slamming through the front door, she went immediately to the telephone to call Susan. Just as quickly, she put the phone back on the cradle. Calling Susan had no worth. She'd only be starting a troublesome rumor.

She stewed, going to the kitchen for cookies, took the package down and then put it back unopened.

If Alicia was involved, Seth deserved to know.

CHAPTER TEN

Seth tossed his cap on the bar and divested his uniform of cell phone, police radio, pistol, belt, badge and wallet on his way to change into civilian clothes. For several days he'd taken life easier, and his back felt better. Not good but better. He could get some work done over at the ranger's house tonight.

Alicia had gone to a youth group get-together at church and wouldn't be home until late. He missed the little monkey when she wasn't around. They'd had lunch together earlier that day and she'd hung out with him, making rounds on the lake until the dreaded boredom struck.

Smiling, he pulled a pair of faded jeans from the closet along with an old T-shirt that wouldn't mind being slathered with paint. His princess was growing up, and from what he'd observed she seemed to be doing all right. He worried about her a lot, prayed about her all the time. A daughter was a frightening thing to a single man.

The smile faded away. He didn't much like being single but that seemed to be God's will for his life. He and the Lord had had a number of conversations, mostly one-sided, about this very topic until Seth had finally stopped arguing the point. But he couldn't say he understood.

He shook his head in self-derision.

The other day he'd all but preached to Kat about the importance of finding God's plan instead of our own. And now he was complaining because he didn't like the direction his own life seemed to be headed.

Regardless of his single status, he was a blessed man. Life was good. He loved his job, had a great church and a number of good friends. He could fish most anytime he wanted, and the view from Kat's cabin would make any country boy drool.

He sat down on the side of the bed and toed off his boots.

This was Kat's house. Maybe that's why he thought about her all the time. He could feel her personality in the choice of deep, comfortable furniture, in the rich, autumn colors splashed here and there, in the warm polished pine of cabinets and trim. She thought she had no gift for decorating, but he knew better.

"Kat," he muttered to the Native American–influenced rug beneath his feet.

What was he going to do about Kat? About the feelings that grew every time they were together?

Nothing, said a little voice in his head.

There was nothing he could do except pray, and he'd done plenty of that. The Lord was probably tired of listening.

His belly growled, a reminder that he should eat something before heading to the ranger's house. A big, juicy burger sounded pretty good.

He stood and stretched his back. A twinge here and there reminded him that he would have to go easy tonight.

In sock feet, he padded through the living room and into the kitchen. A man could stand in this sun-washed room with its wall of windows and stare at the lake forever.

He was putting hamburger meat in the microwave to thaw when someone knocked. He went to the door, his heart leaping in that annoyingly happy manner to find Kat standing on his — or rather her — front porch. She must have cut through the woods on foot because there was no car parked outside.

"Hi," she said, and her smile melted him.

He and the Lord needed to have another serious talk tonight.

Not wanting her to know the effect she was having on him, he didn't return the smile. "Come on in."

He stood to one side as she passed trailing fresh air and sunshine in her wake.

"Did I catch you at a bad time?" She made herself comfortable on the couch.

"Nope. Just got home. I was trolling the kitchen for something to eat." He perched on the edge of the easy chair next to her. If he reached out, he could touch her. He wasn't going to but the thought lingered. "What's up?"

Kat gnawed the corner of her bottom lip. Whatever she had to say must be serious.

"I'm not really sure," she said. "Something is worrying me but I'm not sure if it's anything to worry about or not. Does that make sense?"

"I think so. Is someone bothering you? Someone lurking around your house? A problem for the law?"

"No, no, nothing like that."

She sat back against the cushions and pushed her hair away from her face with both hands in a feminine gesture he'd seen her use a dozen times. He liked watching her, liked the fresh, wholesome glow of her

181

skin, the straight, nononsense hairstyle.

"I'm concerned about Alicia's boyfriend."

"Derek?" Seth frowned, almost relieved to have something pull his thoughts away from Kat and how pretty she looked. Anything involving the kids Alicia hung out with interested him. "What about him?"

Seth listened intently while she told about the encounter with Derek and a friend on the north shore.

When Kat finished, he asked, "What did you actually see?"

"Well, that's the problem." She pushed her hair away from her face again. "I didn't see anything specific. But the boys acted strange and seemed anxious for me to leave."

"Could you smell alcohol?" Forearms on his thighs, Seth steepled his fingers in thought.

"No. I didn't get close enough for that. Although their eyes were red and glassy."

"Could have been from swimming."

She sighed in frustration. "I thought of that, too, but Seth, something didn't feel right. They were behaving oddly. Nervous, silly, cocky."

He tapped his fingers together. "How well do you know those boys?"

"Not that well."

"Could they have been uncomfortable because they don't know you, either? Or maybe they were just boys being boys, acting crazy and showing off." He offered a grin. "We males do tend to show off."

"You won't hear me arguing that point, but I still think something was amiss. You've told me what a nice boy Derek is and yet he bordered on being rude."

Seth frowned. That didn't sound like Derek. "As a general rule, he's a polite kid."

Kat looked up at the ceiling and huffed a loud sigh.

"Okay, here it is straight-out." She brought her gaze back to his. "I think they were drinking or smoking pot. I'm sorry. I don't like to toss accusations around, but I thought you should know because of Alicia."

Man. He didn't like the sound of that. Surely she was mistaken.

"I appreciate your concern." Alicia was everything to him. He expected her friends to be top of the line. "But like you said, accusations alone don't do much. Please understand, I'm not doubting you, but I need hard evidence before I can officially do anything."

"Right. I know that." She squeezed the bridge of her nose and shook her head. "And all I have is a weird feeling."

183

"I know Derek a lot better you do, Kat," he said, intentionally gentling his words. He didn't want to offend her, but he also didn't want to jump to conclusions. "He has great parents. He's a good student, an athlete. I don't like thinking he has everyone fooled."

In fact, he couldn't believe it. Derek was a well-respected Christian boy from a good family.

"I don't either, Seth, but . . ."

She let the thought dangle until he picked it up.

"I'll keep my eye out," he promised. "You can count on it. He's hanging out with my daughter, and that alone gives me reason to be cautious. If anything is going on with that kid, I'll find out."

She nodded once. "That's all I ask."

He could see she wasn't satisfied with his response, but he didn't know what else to say. As an officer, he'd learned never to jump to conclusions. He'd also learned to listen, watch and be alert. And he'd do exactly that.

Kat fidgeted, glanced around the room and then started to rise. Seth didn't want her to go. Especially now when he may have offended her.

"Have you had dinner?" he asked, surprised when the words came out of his mouth.

"Not yet."

"Do you have other plans?"

"Are you inviting me to stay?"

He hitched one shoulder. "We could grill some burgers."

"Do you have any of Mr. Novotny's fresh tomatoes and onions left?"

Gladness swelled in Seth's chest. He was probably setting himself up for a fall, but for now Kat was here. May as well enjoy the evening.

"Sure do. Add a couple of sodas and some crispy potato chips and we'll have a bachelor's delight. I think I have a bag of Oreos in there, too, if Alicia hasn't eaten them all."

She patted her heart. "Oreos, too. How can I pass up an offer like this?"

"You can't. Come on." Grinning like the fool he was, he grabbed her hand and pulled her toward the kitchen.

Work on the ranger's house would have to wait for another night.

Kat sliced ripe, red tomatoes onto a plate, pondering Seth's reaction to her concerns about Derek. She understood his desire not to believe badly about someone he liked. She only hoped he was right. She feared he

185

wasn't, but she'd said her piece and would leave it at that.

"How many burgers can you eat?" Seth asked. He stood beside the sink, smashing beef into enormous patties. Kat found the sight both amusing and pleasant. A man in the kitchen intrigued her. A man who was obviously more competent in the kitchen than she, amazed her.

"You're making those big enough for Paul Bunyan."

"Call him up. We'll share." He placed yet another patty on the plate.

She laughed. "Stop, that's enough. I'll only eat one."

"Then I'll have to eat the other —" he paused to point at each patty, counting "— six."

"Seth! You have to be kidding."

"I am. Alicia will come in later and she'll be starving. I'll eat another one or two for breakfast."

"Still a meat-and-potato man?"

"Some things never change."

No, some things never did. Like the fact that Seth Washington made her smile. In all the turmoil that had ended their relationship, she'd forgotten this feeling of easiness in his company. Though she wasn't sure recalling it was such a great idea. Being with

Seth brought back the other feelings too, of helpless despair, of guilt and shame, of failure.

He took the plate of burger patties and shouldered open the back door. "The grill is hot. Anyway, I smell charcoal and see smoke curling out of the thing. That's usually a good sign. When you finish there grab a soda and come on out."

Plate of veggies and a soda in hand, Kat soon followed him out onto the back deck where the scent of frying burgers nearly made her swoon. "I didn't realize how hungry I was until you started cooking."

"A great chef does that to you." He stood over the grill, poking the meat with a spatula. Juices sizzled on the white-hot coals. Kat couldn't help noticing how good he looked out here on the open deck, so completely masculine but domestic, too. The contrast was both interesting and attractive. Very attractive.

To still those thoughts, Kat unfolded a vinyl tablecloth and covered the small glass-topped patio table. This deck overlooking the lake was one of the reasons she'd kept the cabin in the first place, and the wrought-iron furniture had been one of her early purchases.

"When did you learn to cook?" she asked.

"Mmm, I don't know. A long time ago. I'm a grill man mostly. Steaks, burgers, hot-dogs."

"I'm a microwave girl, but since coming back to the cove, I'm trying to teach myself to be a real cook." What else did she have to do?

He slanted a glance her way. "How's that working for you?"

"I'll never be Susan." Somehow Kat had missed out on the cooking gene inherent in the other Thatcher women.

He flipped a burger. Smoke sizzled upward. "Glad to hear that."

"That I'm not like Susan?" What did that mean?

"Don't get me wrong," he went on. "Susan's great. But so are you, Kat, and not only as a doctor."

She set the vegetables on the table. A frisson of pleasure shimmied through her. Seth thought she was great?

"I can't bake a berry pie."

"Did you ever try?"

Ah, the ugly truth at last. She grimaced. "Yesterday. The birds liked it."

She'd spent an hour cleaning the sticky, stinky mess out of her oven.

He grinned. "Try again. I'm sure Susan didn't succeed the first time she made a pie.

Mom always said baking pies was an art that had to be learned over time."

"True. Like any other skill, I suppose. I didn't learn to insert chest tubes overnight, either."

"Pie and chest tubes, scary comparison." He laughed, shaking his head. "Kat, you have a strange mind."

"You aren't the first who's told me that."

"No, but I may have been the first to notice. Even back in the old days, you were the only girl who ran *toward* the bloody noses and run-over dogs instead of screaming and running the other way."

"I never saw that as odd." She tapped a finger to her cheek, amused. "Which shows how weird I really am, doesn't it?"

"Not weird. Just different. Remember when the football players were keeling over in biology class during dissection?"

"No one ever forgets that. Two hundred pounds of macho male slithering down the wall of the science lab."

"Or when Hog Thomas collapsed in a loud thump on top of the teacher's desk. Papers and pens went flying everywhere."

They both chuckled at the shared memory. Hog, as they'd called him, had been all swagger, a three-hundred-pound defensive lineman who struck fear in opposing quarterbacks. He'd withered like a scalded flower at the sight of a scalpel and a little blood.

"Those poor guys were teased for days," Kat said with a nostalgic smile.

"Yep. And it was all your fault. You were the one who brought in two live frogs and anesthetic. And then proceeded to do a heart transplant in front of the class. Show-off."

She touched her fingers to her lips and laughed softly. More of the good memories she'd lost along the way. "I'd almost forgotten."

"None of the guys have, believe me." He smashed the burgers with the back of a spatula. "Jimmy Jack and Hog rode up to Tulsa with me to see Mom a couple of months ago and told the story to make her laugh. Even she remembered."

The poignancy in his expression touched Kat's heart. From Susan, Kat knew Virgie Washington was in a nursing facility that specialized in caring for Alzheimer's patients.

"How is your mom?" she asked softly. Seth and his mother had always been so close. To see her slowly losing herself must be incredibly painful.

"Doing pretty well under the circumstances. Alicia and I drove up to see her last week. She was having a good day. She told Alicia stories about me as a boy and showed her some old photos."

"I'm glad."

"Yeah, I'm trying to see her every chance I can while she still has good days. Even now she doesn't always recognize me."

Kat's heart squeezed. "I'm sorry. The pain of that must be unbearable."

He gazed down at the burgers as if his thoughts were far away. When he spoke, his voice was low and sad. "She was my anchor, you know."

"I know," Kat said softly, moving closer. She'd counseled any number of Alzheimer's families over the years, but Seth's was the most personal. She truly liked Virgie, a woman who'd raised a fine son in the face of adversity. "And you were her anchor, too."

"Had to be."

He fell silent and Kat knew they both remembered the times Seth had intervened in the spousal abuse that had sometimes landed his mother in the hospital. He'd shouldered the role of protector as a kid and continued today as caregiver.

"Any word from your dad?"

Seth shook his head, his face serious.

"He's still trucking, based out of Kansas City. He stops in once in a while."

"How does that go?" As a teen, he'd despised his father.

"I've forgiven him, Kat. I had to." Seth flipped the nearly done burgers and laid cheese slices on several. The delicious scent sizzled. "I won't say we're best buds, but he's my father, and the Bible says I have to honor him for that."

"I'm surprised. You were so angry."

Seth glanced up. "I didn't say I approve of him, but I honor him and I pray for him. Nothing would please me more than to see my dad find the Lord."

Kat didn't know what to say. His father's abusive behavior was one of the reasons Seth had questioned God whenever she'd tried to witness to him. He hadn't been able to understand why a loving God let his mother be mistreated the way she was.

"Choices, Kat."

"What?"

"I see the wheels turning in that head of yours. You're wondering how I could forgive him after the things he's done."

"You're right."

"Choices. My dad made bad ones. My mom made the choice to stay with him all those years. I tried to get her to leave. She

192

wouldn't. God gives us choices. I made the choice to forgive him. My spiritual growth required it. You can't live with unforgiveness. It eats a hole in you, drains out all your spiritual energy, makes you bitter. I didn't want to be like my dad. So I made a choice."

"Wow." She was impressed. She also knew the statistics on young men who grow up under the influences of abusive fathers. Instead of following in negative footsteps, Seth had become the exact opposite of his dad, choosing to be a man of faith and honor, using his superior strength for good instead of brutality. A woman had to admire a man like that.

"Burgers are done," he said, sliding the browned meat onto a platter. "Mind getting me another cola from the fridge while I dish these up?"

"I can't cook, but I can fetch." She raised her index finger. "One cola coming up."

By the time she returned, the meal was on the table. Once seated, Seth reached for her hands.

"Prayer," he said simply.

She'd known that, but when her hands touched his, her heart thumped and her chest felt tight. She wasn't sure whether it was the man or the prayer that bothered her, but lately both played on her mind more than she wanted.

After Seth's quiet, heartfelt offer of thanks, they each began piling veggies onto a bun, joking about who could grow the biggest burger. Seth won.

All through the meal they talked, mostly about mundane things, a record bass catch, summer baseball, church, progress on the ranger's house. Seth had bought paint and Kat was secretly pleased he'd selected a color she had suggested. She only hoped he didn't live to regret the choice.

When the meal ended and the table had been cleared, they lingered on the deck. The summer air was warm, but a soft breeze blowing in over the lake was cool and pleasant. A perfect summer evening.

"The sunset's going to be nice," Seth said, nudging his chin toward the western horizon. Already streaks of red orange shot up through the clouds to set the sky on fire.

"Glorious."

"Want to sit on the dock and watch it?"

They'd watched the sun go down a million times as teens.

Kat gazed into his green, green eyes and saw that he remembered, too.

"Sure," she said, trying to keep a light note. "I've missed a lot of sunsets in the past ten years."

His crooked smile enticed her. "Grab the moment."

So they did.

CHAPTER ELEVEN

They sat side by side on the end of the dock, shoes left behind, feet dangling as the sun drifted toward China. In the distance someone cranked an outboard motor and the roar slowly eased into the gathering dusk. Along the water's edge, frogs set up their deep, rhythmic mating song. In the trees, crickets added the tenor until night song filled the air.

To Seth, the world felt balanced here on the cove in a way he hadn't experience anyplace else. *He* felt balanced here, which was odd, considering how badly he'd wanted to get away from Wilson's Cove after high school. Now he had no desire to ever leave. There was healing here. He'd come for that purpose and now he'd stay.

Kat. Well, Kat was a different story.

"Any progress on the new business ventures?" he asked, eyes focused on the stunning skyline.

Kat sat close, her shoulder barely touching his. He liked having her next to him, a dangerous proposition to be sure. Kat's intentions were a puzzle. She didn't know what she wanted anymore, but he knew. Sooner or later she'd figure things out and move on again.

"Some," she said. "Todd doesn't really want to sell the marina so I may drop that idea. If I'm going to invest in the fastfood chain, I have to do it soon." He heard the worry in her tone and wondered. "There seems to a time factor and bids involved."

"Are you going to?"

"I don't know."

"You don't seem too sure about anything, Kat. What's up?"

He felt the movement of her shoulder against his as she shrugged.

Seth suspected the answer but he also knew Kat had to find her own way. She was restless and discontented in part because of her estrangement from the Lord. From experience, Seth knew that nothing in life satisfied for long. Only God could fill that emptiness.

"Don't you miss your medical career?" he asked.

She made a small amused sound in the back of her throat. "How can I when someone keeps sending little injuries and illnesses to my door? That wouldn't be you, would it?" She nudged him with her shoulder.

"Me?" he chuckled softly and turned to meet her probing gaze. In his line of work, he talked to so many people every day, ran into injured fisherman and sick campers. Sending them to Kat seemed a sure-fire way to see if she was serious about leaving her beloved medical career.

Her lips turned up in an amused smile. "Yes, you. Or my sister. One of you has to be behind this not-so-subtle attempt to force me back into medicine."

Better now than later, he wanted to say. He didn't, of course. Kat had no way of knowing the effect she had on him. Had no way of knowing the push-pull going on inside him. He wanted her to stay. He wanted her to go.

A hefty bass leaped up, then splashed down again, sending ripples across the water. Golden-red light shimmered and danced with the movement. Nothing was quite as beautiful as a lake sunset.

"Any more problems with that dog?" she asked.

"None. They have him chained now." Even though he didn't particularly like the man's attitude or lifestyle, Ted Shackley had kept his promise to keep the dog under control. For Seth, this was great news. He didn't like destroying animals but he didn't want to see anyone injured, either.

"Poor dog."

"Alicia doesn't think so."

"No, I suppose not."

"I've been thinking of getting a dog myself." He tossed a piece of grass into the lake and watched it spin on the current. "Would you mind?"

"Why would I mind?"

He lifted a hand, let it drop. "This is your cabin. I didn't know how you'd feel about having a big, hairy dog running in and out."

"Oh. I see what you mean. Why don't you get a cat instead?"

"A cat?" He drew back in horror. "Guys don't get cats."

She laughed. "Sadie's mama cat will have her kittens soon. You could take one of those."

He shuddered, an exaggeration but he liked making the serious doctor laugh. "You take one. I'll get a big, ugly dog."

"You used to *have* a big, ugly dog." She bumped his shoulder with hers and laughed again.

"Hey! Don't be disrespecting the memory of a fine canine pal like Bear."

"I would never do that. I loved that old dog."

"Me, too." He sighed, nostalgia sliding over him like a warm blanket. "Remember the time we went hiking up to the rock caves for a picnic?"

"And Bear ate our lunch outside while we explored a cave inside?"

They grinned into each other's eyes.

"Fun times."

"Yes," she said softly. "I'd forgotten how much fun we used to have."

"One bad event can destroy a lot of good memories."

Her face closed up and she looked away, smile gone. Seth wished he'd kept his mouth shut.

"Hey." He tugged a strand of her silky hair and fought down the urge to slide his arm around her. "Look at that sky."

Stunning streaks of pink and mauve on blue were a feast for the eyes as the sun literally went out in a blaze of glory.

In moments the quivering edge of darkness crept toward them. Overhead, in the barely dark sky, the first stars popped into sight.

"I see Venus," Kat said, focused upward, and Seth was relieved to have skirted the issue that always drove her away. They had never talked about it. The topic of their mistake, their shame, their loss and guilt was like a wall between them. Someday they needed to tear that wall down and find a way to heal the wounds. But not now. They'd only recently come together again. Now was too soon.

And he was a coward, afraid she'd get up and leave.

His stomach went south. Was he falling for Kat all over again? Was that what was happening here?

And what if he was? What then? What good could possibly come of it?

The haunting cry of a whip-poor-will sounded in the woods behind them.

He understood the loneliness in that call. Loving had cost him too much but not loving left him empty.

And under the circumstances, he didn't know what to do about either one.

"It's so peaceful out here." Kat breathed in the scent of lake water and moist green woods, letting her body and spirit relax.

"That's what I like about Wilson's Cove," Seth said, his gravelly voice a pleasant burr next to her ear. "It's as if God made this place for the express purpose of washing all the anxiety out of people."

Yes, maybe that was true, but Kat was still anxious, still living in limbo, still unsure what to do. She'd come home but was living in a rented cabin. She missed her work and yet she didn't.

She was also thinking about God more and more, but all the questions remained bottled up inside, waiting to be resolved. When God saw fit to answer, then she'd know He cared.

But the evening *was* lovely, and she planned to enjoy the moment, as Seth had said. How long since she'd done that? She leaned back, eyes closed, hands resting against the rough-hewn wood for balance, and lifted her face to the sky.

She could feel Seth next to her, solid and sure. If she listened closely, she could hear the soft intake of his breathing, feel the rise and fall of his chest.

"Penny for your thoughts," Seth murmured. The sweep of his breath caressed the side of her face. If she opened her eyes and turned her head the slightest bit, they would be face-to-face, inches apart. She swallowed, teetering on the edge.

Better not.

A mosquito buzzed her ear. She swatted. "Missed him."

"She only wants a little bite," Seth said,

tone amused.

She opened her eyes then and there he was. Kat considered scooting away. She didn't. "Then you feed him."

"Her. Feeder mosquitoes are always female, aren't they?"

"Wouldn't you know? The female gets the blame."

There it was again, the memory. *She* was to blame.

Push it down. Don't think about it.

Abruptly she moved sideways and started to rise, reaching out in the shadowy dusk for a handhold. She missed, her foot slipping to the edge of the dock as she began to teeter. Her pulse ratcheted up.

"Seth," she squeaked, grappling now. Any second she would plunge into the lake.

Her body tumbled backward. A strong hand closed around her ankle. Too late. Kat fell backward into the lake. The last thing she saw was Seth's stunned expression as he was dragged along.

A shock of cold water on warm skin hit her like a ton of icy bricks. She struggled to keep her mouth shut, but with no warning, her lungs were empty and she desperately needed air. Flailing wildly, she surged to the surface to suck in a deep breath. Seth surfaced next, slinging water and laughing.

"Brr." His shoulders moved in an exaggerated shiver. "Nothing like a night swim to cool you off. Race you to the other side."

Kat, who'd been prepared to apologize, laughed instead. "You're a goofball."

"We're here. Might as well enjoy a swim." He slapped a spray of water in her direction. She dodged but took a faceful.

"You're in trouble now, mister." She shot back, splashing and pounding the lake with both hands in a disorganized volley.

Seth ducked under the water and disappeared. Kat laughed and kicked her legs. She knew this drill too well. Seth's idea of a good time was to disappear beneath the surface and yank her under when she least expected it. He called it the alligator move.

Dog-paddling like crazy, Kat turned in a slow circle trying to locate him. With faint moonlight to guide her, she saw only the refection of trees and the advancing shadows.

"Seth Washington, you come up right now. Don't you dare —"

He dared. In one powerful yank, he pulled her under, then instantly released. She came up sputtering again, this time laughing, too. He bobbed up in front of her.

"That was for pulling me into the lake," he said. "Payback."

Kat shoved her hair out of her face, treading water and breathless. When had she last done something this silly and fun? "Are we even now?"

His grin was wicked. "Not yet."

Like a stalking shark, Seth began to swim slow circles around her. Kat turned round and round, watching and laughing.

"Be nice, now," she warned.

His grin widened.

"I'll swim for shore," she threatened.

"No, you won't." Moonlight glinted off his smile. "You can't run and you can't hide."

"Oh, you think not?" Kat flipped over and took off swimming. Behind her came the sound of Seth's strokes, powerful and swift. She sped up, trying to beat him, knowing she couldn't. And if she was honest, letting him catch her would be fun.

She slowed, listening, waiting, but he had gone silent. Where was he? She tensed, swishing her legs back and forth, expecting to feel a tug from below at any moment.

Still no sound. Nearing shore, Kat stopped swimming and put her feet down. With the water chest high, she touched bottom. "Seth?"

The only sound was the loud puffs of her own breathing.

Bouncing up and down, she squinted into the darkness across the too-calm lake. "Seth?"

Nothing.

A tingle of worry started up. She pivoted right, then left.

"Seth? Where are you?"

As real concern took root, the water ripped apart with a mighty rush and Seth leaped high into air roaring loud enough to scare the frogs into silence. Water sluiced off him and onto Kat.

Kat squealed, nerves jumping. She batted at him. "How did you do that? I thought something terrible had happened."

Seth was so proud of himself, he couldn't stop laughing — or panting. He'd held his breath for a very long time. "Had you going there, for a minute, didn't I?"

"Yes, you did. I thought I might have to rescue you."

"Rescue could be good." One eyebrow arched. "Mouth to mouth?"

Her stomach dipped. "Oh, you wish."

He moved closer. "Maybe I do."

His gravelly murmur sent delicious goose bumps over Kat's already prickled skin. She couldn't move, couldn't think beyond the fact that Seth wanted to kiss her. Her heart skittered. Wise or not, she wanted him to.

She leaned toward him, aware of his strength, of his soggy, heavy T-shirt, of the heat from his body.

With one wide, water-slick hand, he caressed the side of her face, gently, tenderly. His mouth curved, then parted, his breath warming the chill on her lips.

As Kat's eyelids fluttered closed, the back door slammed and footsteps thundered down the wooden dock.

Kat jumped, eyes opening.

"Dad, are you out here?"

Alicia was home.

Expression wry, Seth leaned his forehead against Kat's for the briefest moment and sighed.

"Later," he promised, then stalked off toward the shore.

"What were you doing out in the lake in your jeans, Dad?"

The trio stood on the deck, Kat and Seth dripping everywhere. He was a grown man, but Seth felt like a kid caught stealing candy.

"Kat fell in. I saved her." He quirked a smile at Kat. Her eyes sparkled, but she glanced down at the puddling water, feeling as guilty apparently as he.

Alicia cocked one hip and eyed them both, rife with suspicion. Okay, big deal. His daughter had caught him about to kiss a woman. It was none of her business.

Self-conscious, he ran both hands down his jeans in a useless effort to get drier.

"Grab us some towels, will you?" he said. "We can't go inside like this."

Alicia stared from one to the other as though she couldn't trust the two adults alone and then whirled away. The door clapped shut behind her.

The deck pulsed with things unspoken. Light from the kitchen poured out like melted butter across the forward sections, leaving the end as dark as the night around them.

Seth leaned against the deck railing and watched Kat bend forward to gather her hair over one shoulder and wring the water-darkened locks. A buoyancy that had nothing to do with the lake and everything to do with Kathryn filled him. He breathed it in along with the moist, fragrant air.

What was she thinking?

"Kat?" he started and was frustrated again when the back door opened and Alicia stormed out.

She tossed a towel at him with a little more force than necessary and then offered one to Kat. "Here."

His daughter's tone needed work. He'd

have to talk to her about that, but not in front of Kat. One thing he'd learned about teenagers. Don't embarrass them in front of others.

"Thanks," Kat said, ever gracious, though she couldn't miss the stiffness in his daughter's attitude. "If you don't mind, I'll return this later. It's getting late. I should head for home."

"Let me drive you." He wasn't ready to let her go. Not yet. He wanted — He didn't know what he wanted.

She shook her head. A small shower sprinkled him. "Not necessary." She smiled then, humor alight in those baby blues. "Thank you for dinner *and* for the swim."

Seth draped the towel around his neck, mouth twitching. "You started it."

She stepped off the deck. "See ya later."

"Let me walk you home." He started down the steps.

She held one hand in a stop sign. "No need."

"There is to me."

"The answer is no, Seth. I'm a big girl who goes everywhere by herself. Besides, you can't even walk in those wet jeans."

True enough. The heavy denim weighed a ton. Still, her refusal hurt a little. Was she afraid he'd try to kiss her again? "You could have drowned me."

With a short laugh and a wave, Kat disappeared into the night.

"Call me when you get there," he said loudly.

Her disembodied voice came back to him. "Okay, officer. I won't talk to strangers in the woods, either. Especially the big bad wolf."

Seth chuckled but stood on the deck for a long time, listening, making sure she was safe. She might be an independent woman and Wilson's Cove was a relatively safe place, but he'd been a cop for a long time and a man even longer. The protective male urges didn't go away.

In less than five minutes, his cell phone rang. He grabbed the device from the deck table. "Are you there?"

"I'm here, safe and sound." She paused. "Thanks for tonight, Seth. I had fun."

"Yeah, me, too." He glanced up to see Alicia staring at him. "Let's do it again sometime."

"Maybe. 'Night, Seth."

" 'Night." He wanted to say a lot of other things, too, but his daughter seemed determined to listen in.

When he clicked the cell phone closed, Alicia said, "What was *she* doing over here?"

Though not certain he wanted to justify his actions to a fourteen-year-old, Seth answered, "We're friends. Although she did have a purpose that I want to talk to you about."

A beat of silence. "Am I in trouble?"

Seth had been rubbing his hair with the towel. He stopped and looked up. "Should you be?"

"No."

"Good. Let's go inside so I can get out of these wet clothes." He led the way, blinking against the bright kitchen lights. "Have you eaten? We have leftover burgers."

Alicia eyed the dishes in the sink. "She had dinner here?"

The third degree was starting to annoy him. "Is that a problem?"

"I guess not. It's your house."

"Actually, it's hers."

"Oh, yeah. I forgot." Alicia went to the fridge and started pulling out condiments. Seth set the plate of hamburger patties in the microwave and pressed the buttons.

"I'm gonna change. Back in a minute."

By the time Seth returned, dry except for his hair, Alicia had settled on the sofa, a plate balanced on her curled-up legs, television on. His heart squeezed. She was a beautiful child even with her shaggy haircut and funky clothes. He prayed to God that she would always be safe from the craziness of this world.

"Did you and your friends have fun to-night?"

"Yeah."

"What did you do?"

She popped a potato chip into her mouth and crunched. "Played video games mostly. After the Bible-study part, I mean."

"Who was there?"

She hitched a shoulder. "The usual."

Seth pulled the ottoman around in front of a fat, easy chair and propped up his feet. "Do these *usual* people have names?"

Body slumping in annoyance, she rolled her eyes. "Yeah."

"Derek?"

"Yes, Dad, you know that. He's the one who brought me home. You said he could."

"Who else was with you?" He'd made a hard-and-fast rule that she could not be alone in the car with Derek.

"I know the group date rule, Dad. Jenny and Cassie and Ben." She plunked her plate onto the coffee table. "Why are you asking all these questions? I was at *church*. You like for me to go to church."

"Because you're my daughter and it's my job to know who you hang out with." He tried to keep his voice calm and reasonable even though Alicia was getting a little testy.

"Now you know." She crossed her arms and focused on the TV.

He waited a minute, gathering his thoughts. He still hadn't asked what he really wanted to know.

"Did Derek have fun jet skiing today?"

His daughter's eyes flicked to his and then back to stare intently at the television. She couldn't be that fascinated by an ad for nasal spray. "I guess."

"Who was with him? Clint and Ben?"

With a loud huff, Alicia pointed the remote and silenced the television. "What is with you tonight? If I've done something wrong just tell me."

"You haven't. Dr. Thatcher saw Derek and another boy on the lake today. She thought they might have been drinking."

She exploded up off the couch, fists tight at her sides. "What a mean thing for her to say! Derek's the coolest guy in town. You said so yourself."

He held up both hands in what he hoped was a calming gesture. "I know. I just wondered if he'd ever done anything like that in your company."

Face belligerent, she bit out, "No."

"If he had, would you tell me?"

"He hasn't. And your nosy girlfriend shouldn't go around saying stuff about people. Who does she think she is, anyway? Somebody special because she's a big doctor or something?"

"Whoa, now. Easy there. Rude behavior won't cut it with me."

She clapped her mouth shut, insult rolling off her in waves. Grabbing her plate, she stomped into the kitchen, clattering her dishes into the sink with more noise than necessary. She reappeared and without a word sailed up the stairs to her room. Seth heard the door shut and the lock click.

Gut twisted into a dozen knots, Seth scraped a hand down his face. Before the divorce, Alicia had been a sensitive little girl. Now she was an oversensitive teenager and he was as lost as a goose in a hurricane when it came to dealing with her.

"Lord, I could use some wisdom."

He didn't want to drive his only child away by being one of those overprotective, suspicious parents. The divorce had done enough damage. The last thing he wanted was to hurt her anymore.

He wished Kat had never come to him with her suspicions, especially since he was convinced Derek was innocent. Well, almost convinced.

■ ■ ■ ■

An hour later Seth sat in the living room with the lights off, head down, clasped hands hanging off his knees, thinking and praying. A man with two females on his mind had a lot to think and pray about.

The evening with Kat had stirred him up, made him wonder if they could somehow fix the broken past and try again. Crazy. He was crazy. She'd never hinted at wanting such a thing. But there was that moment right before he'd moved to kiss her when she leaned toward him, her eyes grew soft and the impossible had slid into his consciousness.

Then the argument with Alicia had just about finished him off. His track record with females spoke for itself.

"Daddy?"

He opened his eyes and glanced up through the darkness. Lit only by the shards of moon he and Kat had admired earlier, Alicia, voice soft and sweet and hesitant, was a shadow hovering next to his chair. He hadn't heard her come down, but she seemed to have gotten over her anger.

"What, baby?"

"Can I have some money to rent a canoe

tomorrow? A bunch of us want to float around the lake."

The quest for funds calmed a lot of teen-age anger. "Still mad at me?"

"No."

He reached up, hooked an elbow around her neck and gathered his little girl to him.

"I love you," he murmured against her gel-sticky hair. "I'm sorry we argued."

"I know. I love you, too." She snuggled into his chest and his heart swelled with a paternal love powerful enough to take him to his knees. "I wish you and Mom hadn't divorced."

That again. Her melancholy tone stabbed him deeper than a switchblade. Talking about the divorce was always a high wire dance. He refused to berate Rita and the terrible wrong she'd done, because some-where along the line he'd made his share of mistakes. Not the same kind, thank God. He didn't have the guilt of adultery hanging over his head, but he must not have been a great husband or she wouldn't have looked elsewhere.

At the same time, Alicia had to understand that there was no going back. Her mother made the choice. She remarried. She turned her back on God.

"We can't change it, Alicia."

"Would you go back if Mom asked you?"

He sighed. "She won't."

He didn't bother to remind her that Rita had a husband. Or that at some point he'd emotionally moved away from that terrible fractured time and the destroyed marriage.

"Is it because of Dr. Thatcher? Is that why you won't try to get back with Mom?"

Caught off-guard, Seth blinked. "What?"

Such reasoning could only make sense to a teenager.

"You and Dr. Thatcher. You're always with her."

"Sweetheart, your mother is remarried. *She's* the reason for the divorce. Dr. Thatcher had nothing to do with it."

"You're not going to marry her or anything, are you?"

Seth laughed ruefully and shook his head. Hadn't he just now been wondering if a second chance with Kat was possible? And hadn't he concluded that he was delusional? "Kat's already married."

He felt Alicia's bewilderment. "Married? To who?"

"Her career."

"Then why isn't she working? Why does she say she's finished with being a doctor?"

Good question. "She'll go back."

They sat in silence, the anniversary clock

tick-tocking away the minutes. Seth wanted to ask more about Derek. He wanted her to promise she'd never do anything stupid or get herself hurt. But they only had the summer, and he couldn't stand to spend their little time together in contention. She'd answered his questions. He had to believe her.

"Daddy?"

"Yes?"

"Can I have twenty dollars for tomorrow?"

He gave a short laugh. "Sure."

She kissed his cheek and bounced out of the chair. "Thanks. I love you, Daddy."

Then her footsteps pounded lightly up the stairs. This time she closed the door with a soft snap.

Seth scratched his eyebrow and stared after her.

He had no qualms about taking down a criminal twice his size armed with an automatic weapon, but with a ninety-pound daughter he had no confidence at all.

CHAPTER TWELVE

"Kat, come over to the house. Quick. We have an emergency."

At the worry in Susan's voice, Kat gripped the telephone receiver tighter. In the background someone was crying. "What's going on? Who's hurt?"

"Just bring your medical bag and come. Now." The phone line went silent.

As quickly as possible, Kat grabbed her things and raced out into the night toward her childhood home. All the while, she fretted. The idea that one of her nieces or nephew was badly injured in this town with no medical facility erased every vestige of her professional objectivity.

Reflected in the yellow bug light, four-year-old Sadie met her on the front porch, squalling and wailing. "Aunt Kat, Queenie's hurt."

Kat was through the door and past the

living room before the child's words registered.

"Queenie?" she asked, slowing her footsteps as she followed the sound of voices coming from the brightly lit kitchen.

Sure enough, the heavily pregnant white cat, wrapped in bloody towels, lay inert on the big round table. Susan stood with one arm around a crying Shelby while Jon gently stroked the mama cat's head.

"Oh, my goodness. What happened?" She plunked her bag on a chair and stared at the wounded cat.

"A big dog caught her," Jon said, blue eyes brimming though he was trying hard to hold back.

"She's too fat to climb trees," Shelby said, voice thick with tears. "We couldn't make him stop."

Sadie, who had trailed Kat into the house now clung to her mother's side. "Can you fix her, Aunt Kat?"

"Honey, I'm a people doctor. I don't know anything about cats."

The answer wasn't what the little girl wanted to hear. Although she'd stopped sucking her thumb ages ago, she chewed on the side and boo-hooed all the louder. "I thought you could. I know you can. Please, Aunt Kat. She's the best kitty in the world."

Kat couldn't deny that. When not so pregnant, the sweet old feline cheerfully suffered the indignity of wearing doll clothes, hats and being pushed in a doll stroller. Kids could do about anything with Queenie and she never got upset.

"Do what you can, Kat," Susan said, as she stroked her baby's dark hair. "She's probably not going to make it, anyway. You won't hurt by trying."

What could Kat say to that? The only vet in Henderson was long closed, and after-hours care didn't exist in small towns. She was Queenie's only hope.

"If she has internal injuries, we're out of luck. But I can clean and stitch the wounds and give her some antibiotic. No promises, though. I'm not a vet."

Susan let out a held breath. "Thanks, honey." Tears welled in her eyes. "Silly old cat."

Kat dug in her bag and found a mild sedative. She had no idea what the proper dose would be for a pregnant cat, so she estimated weight and slid a needle into the animal. Queenie looked up at her with sad, pain-filled eyes that slowly glazed over as the medication took hold. Poor thing.

"I'm going to need some more towels, some gauze or clean rags if you have them, and a pan of warm water."

"I'll get it," Shelby said, face pale. "But I can't watch. The smell is making me sick."

"I'll help you, Aunt Kat." Jon's voice was quiet, but the ten-year-old's eyes gleamed with a fascination she understood. "If you'll let me."

Kat looked from her nephew to his mother.

"He's so much like you," Susan said, pride in her voice. "If he doesn't become a doctor or a vet, we'll all be surprised."

"This town could use both," she told him. "And I can use your help." Not that she really needed a ten-year-old. She nudged her chin toward the box of latex gloves she'd brought with her. "Slip on a pair of those. Then be ready to do whatever I tell you. Okay?"

"Okay." The latex popped and snapped as he struggled into the gloves. Kat suppressed a smile. Later, she'd show him an easier method.

Once the cat was sedated, Kat examined the wounds and went to work, directing Jon to catch the excess irrigation water with towels. No use making a mess of Susan's spotless floor when Jon longed to feel useful.

"Whose dog got hold of her? Did anyone see it?"

"We all did," Shelby said. One hand hovering near her mouth, the other holding her stomach, she looked ready to bolt, but didn't. "Sadie was in the backyard playing with Queenie. I heard the noise all the way upstairs and came down. Sadie was screaming her lungs out."

"I was scared. I thought that big dog would get me. He had big teeth and was looking mean at me." Sadie's lip quivered. "Queenie jumped on him. She saved my life."

Kat figured Sadie was exaggerating but she felt sorry for her little niece. Seeing her cat torn up by a big dog had to be traumatic.

Shelby, who had backed far across the kitchen said, "Jon hit the dog with rocks and finally Mama sprayed him with water."

Kat had wondered how Queenie got so wet. "Did you know the dog? We need to call the owner and find out if the animal has been vaccinated."

"It was that pit bull," Shelby said. "The one that chased Alicia."

Kat's head snapped up. "How do you know?"

"She showed it to me one day when we were out walking around." Shelby shuddered. "He's really a scary dog."

"He's supposed to be on a chain." Syringe in hand, Kat irrigated a gaping wound with saline, fretting over both the wounded the cat and loose pit bull. "Dab that with the gauze, Jon. Susan, call Seth. I've seen that dog in action around people. He's too dangerous to be loose."

Susan, apparently glad for the excuse not to watch what was happening on the table, spun to the phone and dialed.

Kat worked on, cleaning, suturing, thankful for the rise and fall of Queenie's battered little body. She had her doubts about the cat's chances, but for the time being Queenie was holding her own.

"Seth is on his way."

A collective sigh of relief rippled through the kitchen as if Seth's involvement automatically made everything okay.

"How long until her kittens are due?" She started on the final gash.

"Maybe a week," Susan said. "We're not sure. But soon. Do you think they'll survive?"

"If Queenie does, they probably will."

The reminder that even a doctor might not be able to save their beloved pet brought renewed sniffles from the girls. Jon, his jaw set so that he looked exactly like his father, focused on fixing the problem instead of crying about it. Pride moved through Kat as she glanced at her nephew. He really was like her in this respect.

Once all the wounds were stitched, Kat felt for broken bones and found none. Neither did she find any areas where the dog's powerful jaws had crushed internal organs. Queenie had been on the move, sliding away each time teeth had ripped into her hide. "Cats are so limber. That's in her favor."

"Here's a box we can put her in." Susan had lined a cardboard box with an old sheet.

"Can she sleep in my room, Mom?" Jon asked. "I can take care of her."

"Good idea," Kat said. "And if you'd like I'll call the vet in Henderson tomorrow."

"I'll call him," Susan said. She held open a trash bag for Kat to dump sodden towels and rags.

"Seth's here," Shelby announced and hurried to let him in.

The stench of cat fur and blood strong in her nostrils, Kat turned to the sink and began scrubbing her hands.

From the living room came the mutter of voices as the story was repeated. Seth's gravelly rumble punctuated the conversation.

Clean towel in hand, Kat went to join them. As she came round the door frame, Seth glanced up. Olive-green uniform accenting the rich green of his eyes, he looked fit and capable and way too good.

He raised an eyebrow. "Opening a vet clinic?"

She offered what she hoped was a quelling scowl. "Did you find the dog?"

He removed the omnipresent ball cap and tapped it against his palm. "The pit bull was loose, all right. I figure he's responsible."

"What are you going to do with him?"

"I turned him over to the owner. Not much else I can do. He hasn't hurt a person yet and unfortunately cats don't count."

"Sooner or later he will hurt someone, Seth," Kat said grimly. "I remember how vicious he looked the day he chased Alicia."

"Agreed. I warned Shackley again, plus I called the mayor. At the next town council we'll suggest a leash law. After that, I can take legal action if the dog gets loose again."

"Thanks for finding him, Seth," Susan said, hands twisting together in distress. "I would have been afraid to let the kids outside if you hadn't."

"Rightly so. How's Queenie?"

"Holding her own."

"Good."

"Aunt Kat made her better," Sadie said, brown eyes wide as her heart-shaped face gazed up and up at the tall man.

Seth's face softened. He was such a pushover for kids. "I'm glad, Sadie. Your Aunt Kat's a good doctor." He swung his attention back to Kat. "I'm painting tonight. Want to help?"

"What's in it for me?" she joked.

His lips twitched. "I promise not to toss you in the lake."

Kat cocked her head. "I'm afraid I can't make the same promise."

Crinkles appeared around his eyes. "Paint first. Swim later?"

She glanced toward the ceiling in mock disinterest. "Maybe."

"Seven sharp. I'll bring sodas." He pointed a finger. "See you there." He looked at Susan and the kids. "Keep me posted on Queenie."

And then he was gone.

The living room had grown oddly quiet. Kat glanced around at her family's faces. Everyone gazed at her, speculation ripe.

"What?"

Susan raised both hands. "I didn't say a word."

"You didn't have to. And no, there is noth-

227

ing going on between Seth and me. He's helping build my dock. I'm helping paint his house. The sooner he's finished, the sooner I can have my cabin back."

"Whatever. Looked pretty chummy to me."

"Looks are deceiving." She gathered up her supplies, ready to leave.

Susan put a hand on her arm. "Kat."

Kat knew that tone. It was the we-don't-have-a-mother tone, the one Susan used to give advice to her baby sister.

"Be careful."

"Suzie, I'm okay. Stop fretting."

"It's not you I'm worried about."

Susan's words still echoed in Kat's head the next morning as she watched Seth unload his tools from the back of the pickup truck. In all her self-pity, she had never considered how Seth might feel. That she still might have the power to hurt a man who had his life together.

Last night, along with Alicia and a friend, they'd had fun painting the kitchen and living room a soft taupe color. Alicia hadn't been too friendly, but she hadn't been rude, either. Maybe that was progress.

Tonight they would tackle the wood trim with white enamel. After Susan's comment,

Kat hadn't stayed for the midnight swim, but she'd wanted to.

Lumber clattered as Seth tossed the pile onto the dock. "We should finish this side today if I don't get any calls."

"You just show us women what to do, then you can go play ranger." She clapped her hands once. "*We'll* build this dock. Right, Alicia?"

She smiled at the sullen teen standing beside the truck, arms crossed.

"I guess."

"It's gonna be hot today," Seth said. He removed his cap, ran a sleeve over his forehead. "How was the cat this morning?"

"Doing pretty well. She was eating, which is always a good sign, but very, very sore."

"Dad bought some kind of bench kit for you," Alicia said, pushing away from the truck with a look that said she wasn't too pleased to have her father buying Kat gifts. So much for progress.

"Really? Seth, how nice of you." Pleasure warm as the morning sun shafted through her.

"Your first full project," he said. "The dock could use a bench along the railing here," He signaled the spot with his hand. "And the kit looked fairly simple."

Kat headed around to the back of the

truck, eager to see the kit. "Simple is good."

Together they removed the large box and opened it on the grass. Alicia found the directions while Kat laid out the pieces in groups.

"I need to finish the dock before we start on that," Seth said.

"You finish the dock. We ladies will work on this. I'm itching to pound some nails. How about you, Alicia?"

She shrugged. "I guess."

But Kat saw the look in the teen's eyes. She was interested, though she didn't want to be.

She set to work, determined to build both a bench and a friendship. Alicia pretended disinterest, but before long she was hammering and running Seth's drill. Each time their gazes met, Alicia's smile left and anger flared in her expression. Had Seth told her about Kat's suspicions of Derek? Was that why she was even more hostile today?

"Any news on the lawsuit?" Taking a break, Seth popped the top on a soda can.

"Nothing new." She was depressed about the lack of progress. She wanted the problem solved so she could move on. To what, she didn't know. "Any news on the break-ins?"

"None there, either. Things have been

strangely quiet since the Novotnys' house was vandalized."

"Is that a good sign?"

"No trouble for three straight weeks is always good. The consensus around town is that the do-wrongs were summer people who've already left."

"But summer's only half over."

"True. And with the Fourth of July celebrations coming up, we'll have an influx of boaters and campers. I'll be busy enough keeping the drunks from driving boats and jet skis and causing fights on the lake. More reasons to hope the vandals are gone for good."

Alicia, busy screwing a bracket onto the arm of the bench, asked, "Do you think you'll ever find out who was doing it?"

"Sooner or later most crimes are solved."

"But you're really busy, Dad, so if the trouble has stopped, why waste your time looking for them?"

Seth frowned at her over his soda can. "Enforcing the law is never a waste of time. My job is to protect the people of this town. I take that responsibility seriously."

"I know. I mean . . ." Alicia shrugged and dropped the screwdriver. "Nothing, I guess. Is there more soda?"

"In the house," Kat said. "Help yourself."

"Thanks." Alicia whipped around and trudged up the embankment to the cabin. The screen door slapped shut behind her.

Seth blew out a gusty breath. "I asked her about Derek."

"I thought you might have. She was a little chilly toward me."

"Sorry."

"Don't worry about it."

"I do. I want the two of you to be friends." So did she. "Why?"

The question was as much for herself as for him.

He placed a hand on each thigh and laughed. "Because I'm a *peace* officer. Why else?"

She laughed and tossed a sliver of wood at him. He dodged it and laughed again. "You're doing a pretty good job on that bench."

The project was a kit. If she could read, she could assemble a ready-cut bench. "Maybe I'll open a carpenter shop."

"Back to that, huh? Are you ever going to settle on a business?"

She laid aside a bag of bolts. The restlessness was starting to drive her crazy. "Nothing seems to fit."

"That's because you're a doctor, Kat. You spent years getting to this point. You can't just walk away from it all. You're fooling yourself if you think you can."

"Some days I wonder if you're right. I don't know. I just don't know." And she was going crazy trying to decide. "I'm giving the matter a lot of thought." She watched his face for any sign that he cared one way or the other. She couldn't tell. "I've been thinking about some other things, too."

"Such as?"

"I'd like to attend church this Sunday. Will you sit by me?"

This time he let his feelings show. A smile started slow and spread across his tanned face. "I'll even buy you Sunday dinner afterward."

"Good." Her head bobbed forward several times. "Good."

She was a little nervous about attending church after all these years of feeling estranged from God. She couldn't even explain why she wanted to go. She only knew she needed to.

"Kat?" Seth crushed the aluminum can in one hand.

"Hmm?"

"About that kiss the other night."

Her heart beat once, hard. She hadn't seen that coming. "There wasn't one."

Taking aim, he arched the shiny metal

high into the air. The can clattered into the back of his truck.

"I hope I didn't cross any line."

"You didn't."

"Because of the history between us —"

Kat stopped him. "Forget the past, Seth. I have."

She hadn't, but there were some things she could not discuss, not even with him.

He pushed away from the truck and came toward her. "I don't think you have."

She swallowed and stepped back. "I don't know what you mean."

"Yes, you do." He was so close now she could see the yellow glints encircling his irises and smell the sawdust on his clothes. "The issue is there between us every time we're together. A force as strong as a wall. We need to get it out into the open once and for all."

Heart clattering like the pop can, Kat shook her head and backed away. Her mouth went as dry as sawdust. "I don't know what you're talking about."

His cell phone rang. Kat thought she would die of relief.

With a frustrated groan, Seth yanked the telephone phone from his belt and spoke into the receiver, his gaze holding hers.

She felt the heat rush through her, felt the

flush on her skin. Guilt. Shame. Despair.

Why had she thought she could spend time with Seth without paying the price? Sooner or later the ugly past always came back to torment her.

CHAPTER THIRTEEN

Three days passed while Seth stewed about the incident at Kat's place. He'd tried to force the issue into the open, and now she wouldn't even speak to him on the phone. For three days he'd gotten nothing but her voice mail. When he tried stopping by, she wouldn't answer the door. He'd worked on her dock alone, knowing she was inside the house.

The truth was he could have finished her dock weeks ago, but he dawdled, leaving bits undone so he'd have an excuse to see her. Now even that wasn't working. Why didn't he get a clue?

"You're in a bad mood." Alicia tossed her magazine onto the coffee table and glared at him. "I'm going to call Derek and go somewhere."

Seth sat slumped in his chair staring at the tube. He hadn't comprehended a single scene of the show. Alicia's comment only made him more upset.

"No, you're not." The hour was much too late for her to be out with anyone.

"Well, why can't I? It's no fun sitting around here with a grouch. I'm bored."

He pointed the remote and killed the TV. "Don't say bored again. I'm tired of hearing it."

She puffed up like a microwave marshmallow and didn't say anything for several minutes.

Good. He could use the peace and quiet.

"Why are you in such a bad mood?"

So much for peace and quiet. "I'm not."

"It's because of your girlfriend, isn't it? She hasn't called or come over. Did you have a fight?"

He glared at her. "No. And she's not my girlfriend."

She glared back. "Dad, I'm a teenager, not a baby. You like her. I can tell."

"I don't think the feeling's mutual."

"Well, if you asked me, she's pretty stupid if she doesn't like you. You're a hunk." She pulled a face. "I mean, my friends think you are. I think it's kind of sicko for someone to say that about my dad, but anyway . . ."

She gave a tiny, self-conscious laugh that touched him. He softened.

"Sorry. I shouldn't take my sour mood

out on you."

In fact, he wanted to be a Christlike example to his child, not a whining excuse for a father. He rubbed tired hands down his face.

Alicia pushed off the couch and surprised him with a kiss on the cheek. "Don't worry, Dad. I still love you. Even great dads like you have bad days."

"Wow. How much is that going to cost me?"

"Dad!" She pushed his arm and giggled. "Twenty dollars?"

She wasn't kidding. "How about a game of Super Mario instead?"

"Do I have to let you win?"

"What kind of dad would I be if I expected you to let me win?" He hooked an elbow around her neck and knuckled her hair. "No, you don't have to let me win. But I'll give you five bucks if you do."

She giggled. "You're so silly."

"You pop the popcorn. I'll set up the game station."

"Deal."

Feeling better, Seth slid the audio-visual connectors into the front of the television set while the smell of popcorn filled the house.

Alicia came humming into the living room

with a giant bowl of the buttery stuff just as the house telephone rang. With the natural speed of a teenager, she deposited the bowl and grabbed the phone.

"Hello." Her shoulders slumped in disappointment. With a roll of her eyes, she held out the receiver. "It's for you. The woman who doesn't like you."

Refusing to acknowledge the leap in his chest, Seth took the phone. "Hello."

"Seth." Kat's voice sounded strained. Okay, he understood that. He felt a little strained himself, considering the cold shoulder of late.

"Yeah?"

"Can you come over?" There was something more than reserve in Kat's voice, something he couldn't understand.

He frowned, looking from his daughter's face and her bowl of popcorn to the video game. "I'm kind of busy."

A sharp intake of breath. "Someone broke into my house."

Kat leaned against the wall of her tiny kitchen, arms crossed to keep her heart from banging out of her chest. She felt violated to know some stranger had been in her home and had gone through her belongings. There was something creepy about

239

having an unknown person touch one's personal items.

Seth's boot steps sounded as he moved through the rooms. He'd brought Alicia with him and she sat in wide-eyed silence at the table. Kat understood her stunned expression all too well.

"Anything missing?" Seth asked as he re-appeared from the living room.

"A few things from my medical supplies, I think. I keep them in the bedroom closet."

"Show me." He was all cop and very professional, but his voice was gentle as if he thought she might break down. She wouldn't. Caring for broken bodies was far worse than cleaning up broken glass.

She led the way to the bedroom and indicated the sliding doors where a jumble of items tumbled out in disarray.

"The burglars may have been looking for drugs," he said as he snapped photos and made notes.

"I don't keep that kind of thing here."

"They don't know that."

At a loss, Kat slid to her knees in front of the dresser and began refolding scattered clothing. Anything to keep busy and not wonder what would have happened if she had come home during the break-in.

Behind her, Seth headed into the bath-room.

Almost immediately, he reappeared. "Have you looked in here?"

"Not yet. Why?" The minute she'd arrived home from town, seen the open front door and the ransacked bedroom, she'd called Seth, too unnerved to do much exploration.

He hitched his chin toward something behind him, something she couldn't see. With trepidation, she placed a folded T-shirt in a stack and went to join him. She looked from Seth's rigid jaw to the object of his attention, her mirror.

Neatly printed in black marker across the glass were the words Go Back Where You Belong.

Her mouth dropped open.

"This wasn't a random break-in." Seth's quiet voice deepened in anger. "This was personal."

A cold knot tightened in Kat's stomach. "You mean someone intentionally targeted my house to frighten me? Why?"

He carefully opened the mirrored cabinet and looked inside. "Made any enemies lately?"

"Not that I know of . . . Wait. What about Shackley? Word gets around in this town. He has to know I was involved when

241

Queenie was attacked."

"That's a thought. But why you? Why not your sister or me?"

Miserable to have no real answers, she admitted, "I don't know."

"Anything missing in here?" He indicated the medicine chest.

She crossed to the cabinets. In the close quarters, Seth had to shift to one side to make room, but his presence was a comfort. She was definitely rattled.

"Nothing." She turned in the cramped space and found him watching her closely.

"Are you okay?"

"Sure." She wasn't sure at all. She wrapped her arms around her waist and admitted, "Shaken. Now I know how Agnes Novotny felt."

"You aren't going to have a heart spell, are you?" His lips quirked but his eyes were serious. "I know a good doctor, but if you have a heart attack, she'd be out of commission."

Seth's attempt to lighten the mood worked — a little. "I might if I stayed here by myself tonight. I think I'll call Susan. Go over there."

"Good idea. Wait until I'm finished here and I'll follow you."

"No need."

"Humor me. I'm a protective guy."

Relief roiled up inside her. She didn't realize how nervous she was about being alone until now. "Thanks. I'd appreciate it."

"Remember, our vandals are just that. No reason to think they'll become violent."

"Right." At the mere suggestion of violence goose bumps rose on her arms. She rubbed at them, chilled inside. "What else do you need to do?"

"Not much. Give me a minute to walk around outside. Point of entry appears to have been your kitchen window. Wasn't it locked?"

"Probably not."

His scowl told her what he thought of that. He'd lectured her more than once about the casual openness of her house and car. Wilson's Cove was supposed to be safe. It had always been safe. The secure, peaceful existence here was what had drawn her back when life had become too much. Now someone had chosen to destroy that tranquility.

"Get whatever you need for the night," Seth said. "I'll be right back."

Kat found her overnight bag and jammed a few items inside, then phoned Susan.

"Dr. Thatcher." Alicia spoke for the first time, her voice shaky. "I'm sorry this happened to you."

Kat studied the girl's face. There was something there. Fear? Was Alicia concerned about her own safety? "Thank you, honey. Don't worry. Your dad will take good care of you. No one would dare break into your place."

Alicia opened her mouth to say something but then pressed her lips together and dropped her gaze, nodding.

"Let's go, ladies," Seth said, coming in from the back door. "Everything is secure for the night. Did you call Susan?"

"She'll be standing on the front porch."

He smiled. "Ready to do battle for her baby sister?"

"Like always." And the knowledge brought the first press of tears to Kat's eyes. She had let Susan down so many times, but her sister was always there for her.

"Head for the truck, Alicia." Seth held the door open while the women stepped outside. The crescent moon shed a little light so the night was filled with shadows. "I'll be there in a minute."

Kat had never been afraid but a shiver ran up her back. She was relieved when Seth escorted her to her car. The dome light flared as he checked the back seat before letting her inside. She smiled her thanks.

"You really are a cop." She stood in the open car door, facing him. "Thanks for coming over. I'm sorry about the other day —" Kat let the rest die on her lips. How did she apologize without bringing up the topic that had put a wedge between them in the first place?

Seth rested an arm along the top edge of the car window.

"I know," he said simply. "It's okay."

But it wasn't okay. Not really. He knew she'd been avoiding him, but he'd charged to the rescue without hesitation the moment she'd called. A woman had to respect a man like that, a man with the integrity to do the right thing even when it hurt. He put her to shame.

"Still going to church tomorrow?" he asked softly, face serious and, oh, so handsome in the shadowy dome light.

"I've already promised Susan, and you know what a bulldog she can be."

Susan had almost convinced Kat that her problem was more spiritual than anything else. Though she doubted her sister's diagnosis, at this point Kat was willing to try anything to end the confusion and depression.

A smile lit Seth's eyes. "I'll save you a seat."

And Kat felt more ashamed of her selfish behavior than ever. Totally focused on taking care of her tonight, Seth had the grace not to mention that she'd promised him, as well, nor did he mention the tension between them. He was a hard man to resist.

"Okay." The word came out in a shaky whisper.

"Hey." Seth dropped his arm and moved closer. "Are you sure you're all right?"

No, she wasn't sure at all. She was scared and confused and needy. There was nothing she'd like better than to fall against Seth's solid, dependable chest and let him hold her. But Susan's warning and her own concern for this good and decent man held her back. Seth cared about her. She had to be very careful for his sake as well as her own.

Fighting the urge to touch his cheek, Kat slid into the driver's seat and closed the door.

The foyer of Grace Community Church was abuzz with word of the latest break-in. Kat, who'd slept little the night before, felt as if she'd pulled a thirty-six-hour hospital shift. Her eyes were gritty and her nerves jumpy. Repeating the story over and over to each newcomer didn't help much.

The only good thing about the news was that it took the pressure off her. No one seemed to notice this was the first time in years that Kat Thatcher had darkened the church door. Amazingly, the building did not fall down and lightning did not strike her dead. She wasn't sure what she'd been expecting, but the townspeople, most of whom she'd known all her life, were as friendly and normal acting as they were at the Quick Mart.

In heels and a gauzy floral summer dress, Kat looked no different than the other women, but she still felt uncomfortable and conspicuous. The difference, she knew, was on the inside, not the outside. Most of these people had something she didn't, faith in an unfailing God.

The double doors opened and people began filing inside. Seth had yet to appear and Kat told herself not to look for him. Don't borrow trouble, so to speak.

"We're going in now," Susan said, giving her a curious glance.

"Fine. I'm ready." She fought off the niggle of disappointment and let the flow of the crowd carry her forward.

A hand touched her elbow. "Hey, Doc."

Her heart leaped at the gravelly voice. She turned to find him there. "You're late."

"Sorry. Overslept. Someone kept me up late last night."

"You look nice." He did. He was all dressed up in gray slacks and a blue shirt that fit him to perfection.

"You stole my line." His eyes crinkled. "You're the one who's looking good."

"I feel like road kill."

"Me, too, but we look good." With a wink, he took her elbow and guided them to a pew near the front where Susan's family had settled. Again, Kat felt conspicuous walking past so many people. No need to ask where Alicia was. She and the youth group banded together on one side of the triple set of pews.

The service began with songs and choruses, some familiar, some new, but all of them seemed to reach inside her. A deep yearning pulled at her soul. She recognized the source. She'd lived for God once upon a time but so many things had happened to steal her faith. How could He ever want her back again?

The ever-present sense of shame rose in her throat like bitter gall. For all her life's success, she had failed God. He'd failed her, too. Either that or He'd doled out a terrible punishment for her sins.

The fresh-faced preacher stepped to the podium. Seth shifted to share his Bible.

She slid a glance at the man beside her. His face glowed with peace and worship, and she wondered how that could be. He'd made some of the same mistakes she had and probably others she didn't know about. Yet he was solid and strong and committed to God. With all he'd been through, how could he be at peace?

The question struck her like a slap. She had no peace. She had success and money and all the good things money could buy. Yet, deep in the core of her being resided a knotted place as hard as a boulder and blacker than cancer.

As a physician, she wanted to examine the place as she would an abscessed mass. And like any other abscess, a festered wound needed to be lanced to drain away the infection.

"Run *to* Jesus," the preacher was saying. "When the going gets tough, run to Him, not away from Him. He's your comforter, your friend, the One who knows your every sorrow."

Tears clogged the back of Kat's throat as she listened to the simple message.

Run *to* Jesus.

Run to Jesus. The truth hit her like a brick. All she'd ever done was run away.

She'd been so angry. So ashamed. So

confused. Seventeen years ago she had run away to college, to medical school, to a career and away from the boy who'd loved her. Worst of all, she'd run away from God.

She'd thought she'd dealt with the issue of her pregnancy at the time, but in reality she'd shoved the grief aside and run away. Seth was right. The wound had been there all the time, festering. Coming home, being with the only other person who knew about her deepest, darkest secret had brought the wound to a head. This was the barrier, not only between her and Seth, but between her and God. Until she dealt with the abscess in her heart, nothing here in Wilson's Cove or anywhere else was going to satisfy.

Ironic that she, a decisive, take-charge physician had been personally adrift her entire adulthood. And she hadn't even known it.

She squeezed her eyelids tight against the tide of blocked emotion. Not here. Not now. But soon, she had to let it out and face it.

She and Seth needed to talk, to bring their shared past into the open and lance the wound. The idea terrified her. She had no idea what awful thing might result, but she had to do it. Maybe then God could forgive her.

250

CHAPTER FOURTEEN

Kat wanted to talk.

The summer night pulsed around Seth as he guided the motor boat across the glimmering lake. He was running later than usual tonight because of a board meeting after church service. No big deal. He'd made truck rounds already, checking campsites, collecting lake fees, and seeing to security as best he could. One man couldn't do everything in an area of this size.

After last night's break-in, though, he wanted to patrol in the boat longer than usual and keep his eye peeled for anything unusual, especially since Kat had chosen to stay at her own cabin tonight instead of with Susan. He didn't like the idea of her staying there alone. That's one reason he was glad she'd invited him over. But not the only one.

She had been strangely quiet after morning worship, though Seth blamed her behavior on fatigue and stress from the night

251

before. During church he'd asked God to help this brilliant, gifted woman to find her way. If he was honest, he'd prayed for himself, too.

When the time came, he wanted to be able to let her go without a fuss, to want what was best for her, because just between him and God, he was in love with her. Again. Not the crazed, self-serving love of a teenage boy but the solid, steady love of a man. He'd keep that to himself, of course. Last time had about killed him. This time, he'd keep his mouth shut and prepare for the inevitable. He was no martyr.

When church ended, Kat had begged off their planned dinner. Her house was a mess and she wanted to put things to right. Understandable. He'd offered to help, but she'd refused that, too, insisting she and Susan could handle it. At first, he'd been disappointed, wondering if they were back to the cold shoulder, but this afternoon she'd telephoned with a cryptic message. She wanted to talk. Alone.

His chest tightened with the implications. Talk about what? The break-in? Church? Her business decision? Them?

Hope flared like a tiny candle. Fool that he was, Seth wanted this talk to be personal.

He pulled the boat up next to her dock

and was about to kill the motor when movement caught his attention. Soft tennis-shoed steps tapped against the new wood as Kat came toward him. The light from the boat glinted off her dark hair and white shirt, casting her in attractive shadow.

"Hey," he said softly. "Ready for a ride?"

He grasped her elbow as she stepped into the gently rocking boat.

"I haven't been in a boat in a long time," she said.

"Grab a chair." The boat boasted two armchairs that swiveled in any direction, a live well for fish, a built-in ice chest, floor space and storage. Seth preferred the little fishing rig rather than a speedboat because of its versatility. "Sorry I'm late."

"Didn't you say that this morning, too?"

He grinned. "Must be my day for excuses. The board meeting at church ran longer than usual. Dissension in the ranks."

"Trouble?"

"Not really. Disagreement about whether we should spend our money on the Christmas pageant or on missions."

"What was the decision?"

"A compromise. Cut back on the extravagance of the pageant and focus on a specific mission project, such as Christmas boxes for orphans."

"And the board required extra time to work out something that simple?"

"You know how it is." Christians were no different from any family. They bumped heads now and then. He placed his hand on the throttle. "Ready to roll?"

At Kat's nod, Seth slipped the boat into gear and eased out onto the lake. Anxious as he was to know what she wanted to discuss, he didn't ask. This was her party. He'd let her do things her way.

Accompanied by the quiet rumble of the motor and an occasional splash of jumping fish, the boat glided along the shoreline. In the distance on land, the glow of camper trailers and campfires was visible. Sound carried easily on the water. Now and then came the slam of a door or the roar of a starting engine.

After about ten minutes of riding quietly, one hand trailing overboard, Kat said, "You were right."

With her face turned up toward the stars, the moonlight illuminated the long column of her throat. The wind lifted her hair slightly off her shoulders and away from her face, casting her profile into pale iridescence. She looked like a queen from some Greek play.

"I was right? About what?"

She went silent again, but he saw the flex of her throat as she swallowed. Her fingers tightened on the boat rail. Kat was nervous.

Seth suspected then, that this was no conversation about the break-in or business. This was about them, and the topic was indeed personal. The loss of their baby ached between them, unsettled and unvoiced.

Seth had managed to put the loss behind him, or so he'd thought, until Kat reappeared in his life.

Blood pounded in his ears, a steady beat of both anticipation and dread. He had to do this right. As a dumb kid, he'd failed Kat with his silence. Even as a man, he tended to close up emotionally and tuck his thoughts away. He wouldn't make that mistake tonight.

God, help me. Help her.

"You can talk to me about anything, Kat."

"I'm starting to believe that. You've changed."

"I hope so. I was a mess back then."

"I've never told anyone." She sucked in a breath and let the words rush out all at once as though they'd been bottled up for a long time. "About the baby, I mean. Have you?"

Sadness descended, heavy as Houston humidity.

"No one. We held it in when we needed to deal with it and let it go. Maybe that's why the ache is still here." He tapped his chest.

Shifting her focus to the darkness behind him, she pushed her hair back on both sides, letting the locks tumble onto her shoulders.

"I don't know if letting go is possible," she murmured, as much to herself as to him. He saw her doubt, her yearning, her deep need to mend the broken places, and yet she didn't know how. Kat had encountered something her brand of medicine couldn't heal.

"With God's help, anything is possible." He knew the statement sounded trite, but the truth remained. God had allowed him to struggle in life, but the Lord had never failed him. In the agony of divorce, God had been there, comforting and slowly healing the bitterness, helping him to forgive.

When he'd first discovered Rita's infidelity, he'd never thought he could forgive. But he had. With God's help, he had. And with God's help, he and Kat would find healing from their shattered past.

He shut down the boat engine and set them adrift in the middle of the lake. Let the current take them where it would. Nothing mattered right now except this conversation. He rotated his chair, so they were knee to knee.

At her sad expression, responsibility weighed down upon him. Where did he begin? What did he say to make things better?

He didn't know.

"I'm sorry," Kat said after a bit, her gaze flicking up to his and then down to the hands twisting in her lap. "So sorry that our baby died."

The words were barely audible.

A lump rose in Seth's throat. He reached for her fidgeting hands, longing to ease her stress as well as his own. Years of ignoring the sorrow had only deepened it.

"Me, too," he admitted softly. "I was scared to death at first. We were just dumb kids. But when you lost the baby . . ."

"I was so ashamed," she said, gripping his fingers tightly. "Ashamed to be pregnant and then even more ashamed afterward. It was as if I'd wished her dead."

The stark, painful words spoke directly to his own recriminations. Hadn't he thought the same thing?

"Kat . . ." he started.

She shook her head and he saw the tears then, glistening in the moonlight as they slid down her cheeks. "Let me say it all.

Good little Christian girls aren't supposed to get pregnant. I didn't want to have a baby. I didn't want the world to know what you and I had done. I had my life all planned out, college, medical school, a great career. I didn't want her." Her mouth curved in a sad smile. "I always thought of our baby as a girl. And then, when she died, I was filled with guilt because I was relieved, Seth. *Relieved.*"

The last word came out in a sob, and Seth could no more stop himself from holding her than he could stop the sun from setting. He pulled her out of the chair and into his lap, cradling her against his shoulder.

"How terrible is that, Seth," she sobbed. "To be relieved that a child is dead? What kind of person was I to feel that way?"

Tears burned the back of Seth's nose, hot and powerful. He understood all too well. The day she'd called him in a panic because of the cramping, he'd driven her to Henderson to the doctor. They'd been too late to save the child they'd made together. All the way home, she'd sat in stunned silence, white-faced against the passenger door. Neither had spoken a word. He'd felt sorrow and confusion, but even more, he'd been relieved to have the problem simply go away. Of course, it never had. Not really.

After that day, they'd drifted apart, too immature to know how to comfort each other.

That fall she'd left for college. Heartbroken and angry, he'd moved to Houston to find work.

They'd both gone on with their lives, but neither had ever found closure.

He stroked a hand over her silky hair. "I had the same feelings. The very same. Relief, shame, guilt. That's why I couldn't talk to you about it. I thought I was the only one. I thought I was a horrible person and you would hate me."

"Ironic, isn't it? As a physician, I was taught to think of an unborn baby as tissue or a fetus. It's much easier to be objective about a tissue than a child. But our baby was a life, Seth. A little boy or girl who was never acknowledged. No one but us ever knew about her. No one even mourned her death. But she was a person, not a tissue."

Seth's chest ached with regret. For seventeen years, Kat had held this inside without anyone, even God, to help her heal. No wonder she was restless and unhappy.

"I did, Kat. I mourned her. When Alicia was born and I held that tiny pink bundle in my arms, I thought of our baby and I wondered what she would have been like. If she would have had my curly hair or your blue eyes."

Emotions too overpowering, Seth fell silent. Kat laid a soft hand against his cheek. "You were hurt, too."

He nodded dumbly. Yes, he'd hurt too, but he was a man. A man wasn't supposed to let the world see his tears. He buried his face in her hair and breathed in the clean essence that had never changed. The essence of Kat Thatcher, the girl he loved with all his heart.

"Will God ever forgive us?" she murmured against his collar.

He placed a kiss in her hair. "Sweetheart, He already has. Forgiving *yourself* is the hard part."

She shifted in his arms, lifting her face to kiss him gently on the jawbone. "Thank you. For listening. For understanding."

"Are you okay?"

She nodded, her hair brushing softly against his shoulder. "I will be now. I never thought I could discuss this with anyone. Getting it out is more of a relief than I ever imagined."

Seth wanted to say he wasn't just anyone. He was the man who loved her.

Instead, he smiled, though the smile was sad with the painful memories. Tilting her face to his, he placed a kiss on her forehead.

And then because he needed her comfort as much as she needed his, he gave in to the sweet yearning in his heart and kissed her lips.

Kat awakened on Monday morning after the best sleep she'd had in months. Her insides, always whirling and spinning and worrying, had gone as quiet as the morning around her.

Last night's conversation with Seth had been painful and difficult, but the sweetest relief had washed over her once the ugly confession was made. They'd talked long into the night, but after Seth headed home, Kat had sat on the dock in the moonlight and talked some more — to God.

Finally she believed again, both in God and in His forgiveness. As Seth had predicted, forgiving herself had been the most difficult step. Hard as it was, she had to let the bitterness go. God hadn't punished her. She'd punished herself by running away from His love and forgiveness.

Like a lovesick teenager, she touched her lips. Seth had kissed her last night, too, a gentle wisp of a kiss filled with emotion — tenderness, sorrow, compassion — that had left her wishing for more.

As a doctor, she understood the psychological bond that develops between two people who share a traumatic experience. As a woman, she only knew she felt closer to Seth than any other person.

She puttered around the cabin most of the morning, making phone calls, turning down an offer to buy the marina. The fast-food bid was quickly coming together. She'd almost decided to go with it.

To check on the status of the lawsuit that wouldn't die, she made her weekly call to the lawyer's office. After a short wait, the attorney came on.

"Dr. Thatcher, hello. Your timing is impeccable. I have news."

Though tempted to say it was about time, she didn't. "Good news, I hope."

"Mmm, yes and no. Now, before you get upset, keep in mind that you will not have to go to court."

"You settled."

"The hospital's insurance company made the final decision. Let me assure you, I did everything I could to have your name withdrawn from the suit. Unfortunately, our best efforts fell short."

Kat's positive mood shifted downward. "The suit is settled but I'm guilty by default. Is that what you're saying?"

"Basically. I'm sorry, Doctor. I know that

was a matter of principle with you, but we really had no choice."

"And my insurance company will have no choice but to raise my liability insurance premiums." She blew out an annoyed breath. "Is there any recourse? Can I fight this?"

"No. But we can include a letter in the records proclaiming your innocence and your lack of involvement with the patient."

Kat shoved splayed fingers through her hair. The denial of guilt was better than nothing, she supposed. "I'll write the letter."

"Good decision." The attorney's crisp tone softened. "The suit is over now, Kat. Put it behind you and get back to work. You're a fine physician. I have a half-dozen letters here attesting to that fact and any number of people who were willing to testify to your excellence. This doesn't damage your career."

"Just my bank account and my ego?"

"Something like that."

Well, she'd lived through worse. At least the suit was over.

Following a quick wrap-up of business details, Kat disconnected, then sat staring at the pattern in her throw rug. Her lawyer was right. The suit was now history. Though unhappy not to be completely absolved of wrongdoing, she was relieved to no longer have the issue hanging over her head like a guillotine.

She picked up the telephone again and took a deep breath. Today was the day of letting go, of embracing the future.

She dialed her medical director.

Anxious as a schoolboy, Seth knocked on Kat's door. Last night had changed things between them. A change for the better, he thought, although her reaction to him and to his idea this morning would tell the tale.

Long into the night, he'd lain awake thinking and praying. God had been amazingly near, and when the idea had come, Seth believed it was straight from God. He hoped Kat thought the same.

She opened the door and her smile welcomed him. "Hi. I was hoping you'd come by today."

"Yeah? Any special reason?"

She plucked at his arm. "As a matter of fact, yes. I have some things to tell you. Come on in. I made tea."

He had something to tell her too, but anxious as he was, his could wait. He followed her inside and sat down on the faded brown couch. It wasn't nearly as a nice as

the one in his cabin, which actually belonged to her. He was starting to feel bad
about that.

"Did you do okay here last night alone?"
he asked, the break-in still on his mind.

"Fine. No worry at all." She placed their
tea glasses on a rustic coffee table and sat
across from him. She looked a little shy, but
she also looked happier, more relaxed. "I
know you'll want to hear this first. God and
I had a talk last night." She touched her
heart. "I've always blamed God for what
happened, but He didn't make my choices.
I did. Running away from my relationship
with Him only made my problem worse."

She was right. This was far more important than what he had to say. "That's the
best news you could tell me."

"I think so, too, but I have more." She
told him about the finalized lawsuit and
then said, "I talked to my boss at the
hospital this morning."

The good mood dissipated. He had a feeling he wasn't going to like this news. "Now
that the lawsuit is resolved he wants you to
come back to work."

"Yes."

Seth's stomach fell. As many times as he'd
prepared himself for this, he should be
ready. He wasn't.

And then she shocked him off the couch by saying, "I tendered my resignation."

His mouth must have dropped open because Kat laughed. "Did you hear me? I still have to write the official letter of resignation, but the decision is made."

She seemed sincere enough, but caution made him ask, "Are you serious?"

"Yes. And I've decided to buy the fast-food franchise. That is, if my bid is accepted."

He didn't know how to react. Part of him wanted to celebrate, but another part couldn't believe she would really leave medicine for good.

"Well, say something," Kat said.

Did this mean there was a chance for them? That's what he really wanted to say but didn't. Nonetheless, hope, tenacious as a weed, sprouted inside him. "I'm a little overwhelmed."

"Me, too. But it feels good, Seth, to finally make a decision. Last night opened the floodgates for me." She leaned forward and touched his arm, blue eyes soft and serious. "Thank you for being there. Thank you for forcing me to face the loss of our child."

He placed his hand over hers, recalling the purpose of his visit. "I brought you a gift. Well, a gift for both of us, I think, and for —" he swallowed "— for our baby."

Kat went still. "A gift?"

"Last night you mentioned something that really got to me. You said our baby had never been acknowledged. I want to change that. Will you help?"

Her eyes filled with tears. "Of course I will. Tell me."

"Out in my truck is a little plant, a baby-pink rose. I thought we could plant it at your cabin as a memorial."

"Oh, Seth, what a beautiful idea." Kat's hand went to her throat. A tear shimmering on her lashes fell.

Heart pounding, Seth pulled Kat to her feet and into his arms. Today he would make things right for her and maybe even for himself.

On the short drive to Kat's cabin, they talked quietly, and Kat tried to express how much Seth's thoughtfulness meant. She tried but failed.

That this big, macho cop would do something so tender and sentimental moved her beyond words.

Together they walked around her small yard, finally choosing a sunny corner location that overlooked the lake. Only a few feet away, a weeping willow bent her delicate head to sip the water and shed her eternal tears. The setting seemed fitting to Kat. Sunshine and tears, the essence of what this small, unheralded ceremony meant to both her and Seth.

Taking the shovel from his truck bed, Seth dug a hole in the moist black earth while Kat carefully prepared the delicate plant. They spoke little as side by side they knelt to tamp the bush into place, and then sat back on their heels, quiet and pensive.

All the might-have-beens and what-ifs danced in the soft breeze ruffling the tiny green leaves. What if the baby had lived? What if they had married? What if neither had left this tiny town?

The answers were clear now in ways that had been impossible seventeen years ago. They would not be the people they were today, and yet, interestingly enough, God had brought them full circle to face this moment all over again. Maybe to give them a chance to do things right this time.

Seth dusted his hands down his jeans leg. "Will you mind if I pray?"

"I'll be disappointed if you don't," she said, and smiled to see how happy such a simple statement could make him. Without God's help none of this would have been possible.

He grasped her hand and held it between both of his while he uttered a simple, heartfelt prayer, and in that prayer he gave thanks for a tiny life that would remain in their hearts forever and asked for God's peace and healing.

A tear of release trickled down Kat's face as she acknowledged her love for the lost child. She also acknowledged the grief she'd tried to ignore as if a miscarriage was somehow inconsequential.

When she opened her eyes Seth stood very close, watching her. "Are you okay?"

Tears held in for too long continued to fall. "I'm better than I've been in a long, long time." Seventeen years to be exact. "You?"

Using the pads of his thumbs, he stroked her cheekbones as if absorbing her tears into himself. Yet his own eyes were suspiciously moist. "Yeah."

He helped her to her feet and slid an arm around her waist, tugging her close to his side. His stalwart comfort was exactly what she needed, because only Seth could understand the strange mix of emotions racing through her. She wrapped her arm around him, too, and rested her head on his shoulder. Together they stood for the longest time, gazing down at the symbol of their lost child.

A slight wind, ever present from the lake, ruffled the green leaves. Next spring, tiny pink buds would appear, a reminder of new life, new beginnings. Kat couldn't start all over, but she could begin anew right where she was.

A cloud passed over the sun as if God was passing by with a blessing.

"For our little rose that never bloomed," Seth murmured as he touched his lips to her hair. She loved when he did that. She suspected she also loved him. The knowledge seeped into her, as peaceful and lovely as the private memorial service.

She'd needed this closure, this moment of letting go of an event that had colored every aspect of her adult life. She hadn't known it, but it had.

A sweet, cleansing peace descended like a gentle white dove. At long last their baby was acknowledged, and the raw open wound left behind by a tiny, unborn child could finally begin to heal.

CHAPTER FIFTEEN

In the days following the sweet memorial service, Kat and Seth found themselves together more and more. A bond had formed that day over the tiny rosebush and though Kat tried to hold something in reserve, she was failing fast. She loved Seth. But she was scared to death of making a mistake and hurting them both again.

She had made a bid on the fast-food franchise and now held her breath, waiting to hear. She was nervous about starting a new business and the truth was she missed the energy and fulfillment of medicine. Susan would have a field day with that information, saying "I told you so," and it would hurt Seth, so Kat didn't tell a soul. But she thought about it more and more.

Last night she'd even dreamed about the emergency room. A dream, not a nightmare. She attributed the dream to two things: assisting Queenie in delivering six healthy kittens, and a phone call from her former medical director. He'd wanted to know if she was still interested in joining a Dallas medical group to which she'd applied months ago. They had phoned him for a reference. She'd been stunned, having put the application out of her mind after waiting so long to hear.

What if they offered her a position? Would she take it?

She honestly didn't know.

"Your pie looks awesome," Seth said, interrupting her train of thought.

Kat was glad. Today was the annual Fourth of July celebration, a major event in Wilson's Cove, not a day to fret about something that probably wouldn't happen, anyway.

"If it makes you sick I promise to provide free medical care." She'd spent all afternoon, with Susan's help, baking the pie.

With a grin, he took the covered dish from her hands and placed it on one of the folding tables set up under the canopy of shade next to the lake.

"I'm holding you to that promise. And I can be a very demanding patient."

"Shots," she countered. "I'll give you lots and lots of shots. Maybe start an IV, too, or do exploratory surgery."

He made a terrible face. "That's why I promise not to get sick." He motioned toward the lake's edge where several anglers were casting lines into the water. Red, white and blue streamers fluttered from the dock along with an enormous American flag. "Want to fish? I brought reels and bait. The fireworks won't start until dark."

Annually, Wilson's Cove sponsored a fireworks display out on the water that brought people from miles away. The town had been a-hum with activity since yesterday. Boats crowded the marina, campers lined the campgrounds, and the pop-pop-pop of firecrackers occasionally startled everyone in hearing distance.

Kat pointed to a clearing roped off with still more red, white and blue streamers. She wasn't in the mood to fish. "We could watch the races."

Part of the festivities included all kinds of silly races — egg toss, sack races, hoop races, and even a wheelbarrow race. Kids of every age competed for small prizes donated by merchants, though mostly they competed for fun.

"Watch them?" Seth said, starting that direction. "I want to participate."

Kat held back. "You have to be kidding."

"Come on. Be a sport. Be my partner."

His partner. That sounded good. A tingle of energy zipped through her. "You're living dangerously, Mr. Washington."

"You only go around once. May as well. Just think, we might win a chocolate-dipped cone from the Dairy Freeze."

"Yippee," Kat said, laughing at his silliness.

"I knew the word *chocolate* would win you over. Let's go." With a tug on her hand, he took off jogging toward the contestant area. Kat had to run to keep up with his longer stride. Once there, she was winded, a fact that did not bode well for the coming competition. But they declared their entry, plunked down the dollar fee and accepted a feed sack, the only needed equipment.

Kat glanced around at the other contestants laughing, hobbling together with one leg each in a gunny sack, having a silly time in general. "We really should have practiced in advance."

"Perfectionist. Where's your sense of adventure?" He held the bag open. "Come on. Try it. We'll make an awesome team."

Kat stuck one foot into the sack next to his much-longer one. They now formed a single unit of two people with three legs between them. Each held to one side of the bag and tried to walk together to the starting line.

"Left, right, left, right," Seth said.

Off balance, Kat giggled. "We're going to kill ourselves. Look how far we have to run in this thing."

At least a dozen other contestants gathered behind the white-chalked starting line, chattering and practicing the three-legged walk. Twenty-five yards further down another chalk mark represented the finish line.

"Easy as pie, sweetheart," Seth said, grinning from ear to ear.

"Then we're in big trouble, because I know from recent experience that pie is *not* easy."

Someone shouted, "On your mark."

Kat jumped. "Oh, my goodness. Here we go."

"Get set."

Adrenaline shot into her veins. She gripped the edge of the gunny sack.

Seth winked at her. "Outside foot first."

She nodded.

"Go!"

The two of them sprang away from the starting line with all the grace of a broken wheel. Kat tried her best to keep up with Seth's longer strides, and he tried to slow down for her sake. The results were an awkward, unbalanced Charlie Chaplin shuffle instead of a race.

But the other contestants had the same problem. As a result, shouts of laughter and groans echoed up and down the line.

Onlookers gathered on each side of the race area shouted encouragement to their favorites. Above the noise, Kat heard, "Go, Doc, go." If she'd had time to enjoy it, the camaraderie would have warmed her heart.

Someone snapped a photo, and the distraction was exactly what Kat did not need. Already unsteady, she faltered as Seth took a giant step. They went down like two wounded ducks, floundering and flapping and grappling to hang on.

"A doctor, a doctor," Seth cried. "I need a doctor." He laughed so hard, Kat could barely understand him. She laughed, too. And laughed and laughed as they thrashed around, trying to sort out which feet and knees belonged to whom.

From her vantage point on the green grass, Kat saw that half the other contestants had suffered the same fate. A few stragglers stumbled on toward the finish line.

"They're going to win my ice cream cone," she moaned in mock despair.

Still laughing and breathless, Seth managed to untangle them and helped her to her feet. "I think all my parts are intact.

How about you? Any broken bones?"

Brushing at the grass stains on her capris, Kat shook her head. "I can't believe you talked me into that."

He grinned, not the least bit sorry. "Ah, admit it. You had fun."

"Do I have to?"

"Yep."

"Or what?" She was flirting and it felt good.

"Or I'll enter us in the wheelbarrow race."

She jerked away in pretend horror. "I had fun! I had fun! No more humiliation for one day, please."

Laughing, Seth looped an arm around her shoulders and snugged her close to his side. He looked down with his sincere eyes, and something shifted inside her, some wonderful buoyant emotion that bordered on hope and centered on love.

No matter Susan's insistence that Kat could never be happy in Wilson's Cove, she was happy today. Maybe there was a chance for her and Seth.

When they stopped to chat with a group of friends, the warm friendliness that made Wilson's Cove a special place wrapped around her like loving arms. Though she'd run away before, she loved this town. Why had she taken so long to recognize the truth? A smile bloomed on the inside. Seth. Most likely, she'd been waiting for Seth. And if the idea of opening a fast-food franchise wasn't as intellectually satisfying as practicing medicine, she'd learn to deal with it.

She hoped.

Kids along the waterfront chose that moment to set off a volley of minirockets, forcing Seth to play his role as policeman. No explosives were allowed near the picnic except those provided by pyrotechnic experts. Kat went with him and watched as he handled the situation in a firm but friendly manner that had the kids apologizing and promising to do no more.

No wonder she was falling in love with him again. He worked hard to be a real Christian. He was such an amazing person and more than one single lady had sought him out today. Yet, he'd always come back to her.

Hours later, after too much food, Seth sat next to Kat on a quilt she'd spread on the ground. They'd chosen this spot on a slight rise away from the rest of the noisy crowd to talk and watch the coming fireworks display.

"Your pie was awesome," he said, patting

his too-full belly.

"It was, wasn't it?"

Seth was amazed by Kat's genuine surprise. The brilliant Dr. Thatcher couldn't believe she'd successfully baked a pie. Her lack of confidence in some areas was both endearing and disconcerting. How could such a brilliant woman not know her own strengths?

"Considering how fast every piece disappeared, I'd say I wasn't the only one who thought so." He patted the spot next to him. "You could move over here a little closer. The fireworks are about to begin."

To his pleasure, she scooted up close to his side. They'd had a great time today. If he hadn't already been in love with her, he would have been after this picnic.

He'd tried to stay away from her. He'd done his best not to fall in love with her. But he'd done it, anyway.

Now that she seemed determined to buy a business and stick around, he was crazy enough to believe they could finally be together. Or maybe he was just crazy.

He dropped an arm over her shoulders. The sun had set, but the warm, July night pulsed with activity. People milled around the lake's edge, waiting for the fireworks to start. The jet skiers had come ashore, and boaters had cut their motors.

He glanced around for his daughter and spotted her immediately with a crowd of teenagers lining the fishing dock, feet dangling in the water. He felt a little guilty for wanting to be alone with Kat, although Alicia didn't want to hang out with him, anyway.

He wished she and Kat could become friends. They were cordial enough but not friends. Alicia seemed to view Kat as a rival, and he didn't know what to do about such an erroneous viewpoint. Kat was trying, and he loved her for making the effort. At Kat's insistence, the two of them had worked together on the bench kit. That had gone pretty well, and Alicia had declared a new interest in woodcraft. Since then Kat had offered to take Alicia and Shelby to the shopping mall in Henderson. He hoped they'd go.

If he was going to marry Kat, they needed to be friends.

The idea hit him in the solar plexus. He wanted to marry Kat. He shouldn't be surprised. They'd been moving in this direction all summer.

His deep sigh had Kat turning her head toward him. "What was that for?"

An enormous starburst of red exploded in

the sky above. Kat's eyes gleamed in the faint glow, searching his.

"Just thinking."

"About?"

He wanted to tell her. With all his heart, he wanted to take her in his arms and pledge his love.

Coward that he was, he snugged her close to his side and murmured, "I think you know, Kat. I think you know."

That was the best he could do for now.

CHAPTER SIXTEEN

Seth tossed yet another empty can into a trash sack. All along the coastline a team of volunteers did the same, picking up yesterday's Fourth of July trash. What had been beautiful and fun in the dark wasn't so pretty in the stark sunlight.

He wiped the back of his gloved hand across his forehead. Noon was still an hour away and already the sun blazed overhead. If the temperature reached the predicted century mark, he'd have to adjourn the cleanup until later in the evening.

"Dad!" Alicia called, waving something in the air. She and several other girls strolled through a grove of trees with their black garbage bags. "I found a twenty-dollar bill!"

He waved back. During cleanups, someone inevitably found money and other valuables. He never quite knew what to do with items such as money, whose owners couldn't be clearly identified. He'd come to the conclusion that the only perk of volunteering was the treasure one might find. He kept a lost-and-found box in hopes that the rightful owners would come in search of watches, wallets, jewelry and other items. Sometimes they did. Mostly they didn't.

"Put it in church on Sunday," he called. That's what he did with any cash he found.

"Okay," she called back.

He stood watching her for a few minutes, proud of his daughter. Being here for more than a month had changed her. She'd lost some of her attitude, not all but some, and she didn't seem quite as tormented by the divorce. She was a great girl and he was thankful Rita had allowed her to spend the summer in Wilson's Cove. She'd needed this time with him. He saw that now. A girl needed a father every bit as much as a son did.

He picked up a wad of fire-blackened paper and a handful of burned-out smoke bombs. Half the town had kept colored smoke floating overhead last night, ostensibly to keep the mosquitoes away.

His spirits lifted as he thought about last night. While he'd sat on the quilt with his arm around Kat, watching the night sky light up in celebration of freedom, contentment had melted over him. More and more, he became convinced that things would work out between them. Though he'd been certain she'd return to Oklahoma City and her career, she was still here, still declaring her intention to buy a business and move back into her cabin for good.

Last night he'd hesitated, but today he was going to surprise her. He was going to give back the cabin and ask her to marry him.

Footsteps crunched on the gravel paths leading from the parking area. He glanced up and smiled. The Lord was treating him especially well today. Kat, in yellow capris and a white shirt, swung toward him.

As she drew close enough for him to see her face, Seth's smile faded. She looked . . . different.

" 'Morning," he said.

"Hi." She looked way too serious.

He closed the top of the garbage bag and tied the orange ribbons. "What's up?"

"Something I want to talk to you about. Some news."

Tossing the bag into the back of his nearly loaded truck, he said, "Good or bad?"

"Depends on your point of view, I suppose. I don't know yet." She hovered close, biting at her lower lip, hands fidgety. Whatever the news, Seth suspected he wasn't going to like it.

His good mood sank to the bottom of the lake. "Want to go somewhere and talk?"

"Let's walk, okay?"

With a tilt of his head, he stripped off his gloves, tossed them into the truck, then fell into step beside her. She led the way down a wooded trail, ambling, thoughtful. Something heavy was on Kat's mind.

She picked an orange wildflower and fiddled with it. "These are beautiful."

He picked another and slid it into her hair. "The cove is a beautiful place."

She nodded, a little sad and pensive.

Seth's pulse kicked up. Anxiety tightened his belly.

"I had an interesting phone call this morning," she said, her face turned upward into the dappled light coming through the trees.

His anxiety increased. "Anything wrong?"

Kat paused, inhaled deeply and said, "A few months ago I applied for a position in Dallas. Southwest Family Care had an opening. A dream job. I really wanted it but so did a number of other physicians. With all that happened afterward — the lawsuit, quitting my job, starting a new business — I put the application out of my mind."

And then he knew. The death knell sounded. "They offered you the position."

She stopped in the trail and faced him. "Yes."

Seth kept his expression composed and calm, though he wanted to throw back his head and howl like a wounded coyote. Ten minutes ago he'd been planning to marry the woman. Now she was telling him goodbye.

His chest hurt bad enough to call 911. He clenched his teeth against the swelling tide of emotion.

If there was one thing he'd learned, first from Kat and then from his failed marriage, a man couldn't force a woman to choose him. Regardless of how much he hurt to lose her again, he still wanted to see Kat happy, to watch her achieve her goals and dreams, even if they didn't include him.

"Southwest Family Care doesn't know how lucky they are," he said softly.

She touched his cheek, eyes searching his. "I don't know what to do."

"Do what you love." There. Simple enough. His heart thudded with the need for her to say she loved him. She chose him. But he was no fool. He'd walked this path before.

"Can't a person love more than one thing?" She looked so uncertain and worried that he pulled her into his arms. She came easily as if she'd been longing for him to do exactly that. At least, he wanted to think so.

"You have to decide what you want, Kat. If you want the fast-paced city life, take the job." Part of him longed for her to ask him to go, too, even though he wouldn't. Not only did he belong here in the cove, he couldn't play second fiddle to her career again. "You'll be great at it. You miss your work. That's why you're still so uncertain about taking the franchise."

"I know. I realized that this morning when Dr. Walters called."

Seth drew in a deep breath, his chest rising. "Then there's your answer."

"I'm useless here, Seth. All I know is medicine."

He wanted to say Wilson's Cove needed medical care, too, but they'd already had that conversation. He was pathetic enough already. No use begging.

He stroked a hand over her soft hair, relishing the feel, mentally cataloging the texture and scent for the hard days ahead. "When are you leaving?"

She pulled back from him then and studied his face. She seemed to be searching for something he didn't understand.

"I asked for a few days to think about the offer."

Seth wanted to take hope in that, but he knew better. She'd accept the offer. She would leave. He would stay. And with God's help, he would be man enough to be happy for her.

Kat was a wreck.

All afternoon she'd walked around the peaceful lake and woods, searching for answers. The day was gone and still she was no closer to a decision.

She'd wanted Seth to ask her to stay. He hadn't. On the night of the Fourth, she'd realized he loved her, though he didn't say so. She knew it as surely as she knew her name. But today when she'd asked his advice, he'd told her only to do what she loved. That was the trouble. She loved him and this town, but she loved the adrenaline rush and the intellectual stimulation of medicine too.

And now, for the past hour she'd driven aimlessly, letting the slow drift of uncongested traffic in Wilson's Cove flow by. She passed houses where people she knew and a few she didn't stopped what they were doing to lift a hand and wave. She'd waved in return, part of a community where farmers and fisherman leaned on the back of pickup trucks to shoot the breeze. Life was different here, slower, laid-back. Some would call it backward, less progressive. In many ways they would be right, and yet in ways that meant the most, Wilson's Cove outshone the rest.

Night had long since fallen, though she had no idea of the time. She parked her car in the dark lot away from the flickering fluorescent lights outside the Dairy Freeze. The old-fashioned establishment had a walk-up window as well as a much-larger inside area where kids hung out to play video games and meet other kids, a blend of progress and the past.

Kat's stomach growled, but she didn't feel hungry. She felt confused.

The idea of joining a busy Dallas medical team held a certain appeal. She missed the work, missed using her skills to help people, missed being busy all the time, but she didn't miss the loneliness, the stress, the terrible hours. Until this summer, she'd had no time for a real personal life since college. Now that she'd found Seth again, leaving Wilson's Cove made no sense.

But neither did leaving medicine and giving up everything she'd worked so hard to gain.

Was it possible to have both? Common sense said no. She was an all-or-nothing kind of gal, total focus on the goal. The only area of success in her entire life was intellectual and that meant medicine. She'd failed at everything else. Everything. Wasn't the youthful disaster with Seth proof of that?

But being with him again, facing the mistakes they'd made, had given her hope that perhaps they could work things out.

With a moan, she leaned her head on the steering wheel and did what she should have done all along. She prayed.

After a long time she sat back and dried damp eyes. Some of the heaviness had lifted, but she was no closer to a decision than before.

She pushed the car door open and headed for the walk-up window to order one of Cherry Clausing's homemade hamburgers. A smattering of cars and trucks were parked here and there on the gravel parking space, and popular music vibrated the walls. Couples holding hands came and went inside the building. Two boys sat on the tailgate of an old pickup flirting with the girls who came past.

The familiar sight brought a smile. Saturday night in Wilson's Cove hadn't changed all that much.

Not interested in joining the noise inside, Kat ordered a burger to go and waited by the window, watching the perennial mating dance of teenagers.

Through the clear plate glass, she spotted Alicia. No surprise there. Seth's daughter was with the usual gang of kids, including Shelby. They were behaving like typical teens, laughing and flirting while sipping sodas or maneuvering video joysticks. Harmless fun.

The rich odor of grilled beef drifted out as Cherry pushed Kat's order through the window and received payment. Paper bag crinkling in her fingers, Kat turned and bumped into a tall teenage boy about to enter the café.

" 'Scuse me, Doc."

"Derek, hi."

He giggled. Not laughed. Giggled.

High was the operative word. Eyes red and glassy, the boy fidgeted and twitched, his behavior overactive and uncharacteristically goofy. He might fool some people, but she'd seen this too many times.

"Derek, have you been drinking?" Or smoking pot, more likely.

"Me? No way, Doc." He towered over her, a smirk on his face. "Heard your house got

291

broke into. Someone trying to scare you off?"

Kat frowned. Why would he bring that up? "I don't scare easily."

"Maybe you should." Still grinning, he patted his chest and backed away. "Gotta go. You take care now, ya hear?"

The boy went inside, leaving her to wonder about his strange behavior. Worried, but not knowing what to do, Kat took her food and headed to the car. Without a doubt, Derek was high on something. Even if Seth didn't believe her, she had to mention her suspicions again.

As she backed out of the parking space and pulled onto the highway fronting the Dairy Freeze, she cast one final glance toward the establishment.

What she saw sent pure terror racing through her veins.

Alicia and two other teens had come out the door and were getting into a red truck with Derek. And he was driving.

Before Kat could react, the truckload of kids pulled onto the highway, tires squealing as they roared into the darkness.

Kat followed, fishing in her bag for the cell phone while squinting toward the red taillights. The roads around the lake were curvy, hilly and heavy with vegetation. Very quickly the red truck was out of sight.

Dismayed, she whipped to the shoulder and punched in Seth's number.

"Washington."

"Seth. It's me. I just saw Alicia with Derek. I'm sure he's high. I'd stake my medical license on it." He hadn't believed her before. She had to make certain he did this time. The safety of four kids depended upon her. "Please, Seth, you have to believe me this time. Alicia may be in danger."

A beat passed. "Where did you see them?"

The tension in his voice was evident. Kat went weak with relief. He believed her.

"Leaving the Dairy Freeze, traveling south in Derek's truck. He was going really fast."

"He was driving?" A cop didn't need anyone to tell him of the danger for an intoxicated, speeding driver.

"Yes."

A sharp intake of breath. "I'm headed for my vehicle now. I'll call her cell, but I'll also drive around and see if I can locate them. I don't want her in that truck."

"I'll drive around, too." Although she didn't know how she'd stop a truckload of kids, she needed to do something proactive. As she started to press *end,* Seth's voice stopped her. "Kat."

"Yes?"

"Pray."

More than an hour passed without any sign of the red truck. As the minutes ticked away, Kat begin to wonder if she'd overreacted. She had already been upset, and her previous encounter with Derek had left her suspicious.

"No," she said grimly to the dark empty road ahead. Derek *had* been under the influence. She was positive.

Hopefully, the kids had gone to someone's house and parked the truck. That was the case scenario Seth had offered when he'd last contacted her, though he was troubled that Alicia was not answering her phone. Kat was troubled, too, but she prayed he was right and they had stopped at friends, leaving the cell in the truck. It happened all the time. Seth was in the process of calling or driving to the homes of Alicia's friends now.

Kat took another graveled side road where dense underbrush crept onto the lane from the encroaching woods. Few people lived back up in here, but she drove the road anyway, seeing nothing but a raccoon.

She and Seth both knew every inch of land around the lake. The problem was the number of roads. They could drive all night and never cover them all.

Another half hour passed and she reached for her cell phone. The device jangled in her hand. She jumped, her heart thudding. In the light of the caller ID was Seth's name.

She pressed the speak button, hoping. "Seth?"

"I just got a call." From the ragged sound of his breathing, Kat tensed. "There's been an accident. I'm heading that way now. Can you meet me? We need your help."

"Where?"

He named the place, less than two miles away.

"I'll be there in five minutes."

His parting words, spoken with a father's terror and cop's calm, sent chills down her spine. "Hurry, Kat. It sounds bad."

Sweat broke out over Kat's body as she drove as quickly as prudent around the curves toward the accident. Visions of that last night in the emergency room played in her head.

Please God, please. Not that. No more carloads of dead teenagers. The implication of a serious accident in this rural location far from a medical facility was frightening to say the least. She had little in the way of equipment for anything truly life threatening.

Up ahead, car lights illuminated a mangled red truck turned on its top. Three other vehicles were parked at angles toward the ditch along the narrow road, their lights on. One was Seth's. A handful of shadowy people hovered over two figures lying inert on the ground.

Kat's heart stopped, then started again, hammering wildly. Adrenaline slammed into her veins as she grabbed her medical bag from the back seat, barreled out of the still-rocking Toyota and ran.

"What have we got?" she called.

"Two look okay, just banged up." Kat recognized the man, Tim Tyler, who lived a good five miles away. Odd to see him here. "That one over there has a broken leg, I think. It's the girl that's hurt bad."

He pointed toward Seth, on his knees beside a girl. Alicia.

"Kat," Seth said, and the look on his face broke her in two. "I think she's . . ." His voice choked. "Oh, please God, help her."

Another surge of adrenaline jacked into Kat's veins. She fell to her knees beside him, making a fast assessment. Airway. Alicia was not breathing. Blood trickled from her mouth and nose. Kat felt for a carotid pulse, found it faint. She also found the probable cause of respiratory failure. The cartilage below the Adam's Apple was sunken, and crackled beneath her fingertips. Possible fractured larynx. Without a scope or X-ray, a perfect diagnosis was impossible, but Alicia didn't have time. Kat had to act and act now. The only recourse was to open a hole in the throat, a cricothyroidotomy.

Maintaining an outward calm she didn't feel, Kat dug quickly in her bag for anything to work with. A scalpel from a suture tray, alcohol swabs, gauze, gloves. Dear God, what could she use for tubing to keep the airway open? She needed an endotracheal tube but didn't have one.

As if the Lord dropped the answer into her head, she reached for a syringe and discarded the inner plunger. It's all she had. It would have to do.

Suddenly Derek stumbled up beside her. His eye was swelling shut, but otherwise he appeared unharmed. "She'll be okay, won't she, Doc? You gotta make her okay."

With no time for niceties, Kat said, "Someone get him out of the way. Keep him calm until I have time to look at him."

She ripped the suture tray open and slid her hands into the latex gloves.

"I'm sorry. You gotta believe me, Seth." The boy's voice broke on a sob. As angry as Kat was, she felt sorry for him. Dumb kid.

But she'd been a dumb kid once herself.

Seth was too focused on his child to answer, but the other man spoke up. "You shouldn't a been breaking into people's houses for the fun of it, you little jerk."

Fingers feeling for the soft spot on the anterior neck, Kat absorbed the awful news. Derek and his friends were the lake vandals. Tonight Alicia had been with them. Dear Lord.

Alicia's unconscious body jerked. Time to hurry.

Kat had never prayed during a procedure, but she prayed now. She'd never been scared before, either, but this time she struggled to keep her hands steady and her mind focused.

With everything in her, she prayed to save Seth's child. She hadn't saved the first one, but with God's help she could save this one.

She relocated the soft spot with one finger, deftly made an incision and then flipped the scalpel around, using the wide end to maintain the opening.

As she worked, silent tension thick as the night around her, something began to stir deep inside. An understanding, a clarity that hadn't existed before. She was a physician, a healer, the only person for miles who could save Seth's child.

As if watching from a distance, she saw her own gloved hands slide the opened syringe into place, saw herself breathe into it, not once but over and over until she heard the sound of Alicia's spontaneous air intake.

In the distance, sirens wailed, a beautiful sound to Kat. The sooner Alicia was in a hospital, the better chance she had of making a full recovery.

One hand holding the tube in place, Kat rested back on her heels to wait for the ambulance. Sweat bathed her face, and her shoulders ached from the strain. She looked into Seth's beloved eyes and said, "She's going to be okay, Seth. I promise."

A powerful gratitude welled in her chest. Thank you, Father God. Thank you for this gift. Thank you that I was here in this place tonight to do Your handiwork. Thank you that I could do this for Alicia and for Seth.

Nothing was as fulfilling as this. Why had she ever thought she could leave medicine? This was her calling from God. This was who she was, who she was always meant to be.

She glanced into Seth's haggard face, loving him more than she'd thought possible. Loving in the way God had intended a woman to love a man.

And as surely as if she'd awakened from a long nightmare, she saw the truth of her calling. She was not only called to be a physician. She was called to be a woman, a friend, a sister, a wife.

God never intended for work to take the place of a personal life or a relationship with Him. That's where she'd gotten off track. An all-or-nothing kind of woman, she'd thought doing one thing exclusively was the only way. How foolish she'd been. How utterly selfish.

"God forgive me," she silently prayed. "I have been terribly blind in so many ways. When this is over, help me to make things right."

God had given her this gift of healing hands. He'd also given her the gift of love for Seth Washington.

If only she wasn't too late. . . .

CHAPTER SEVENTEEN

Seth stared at his clasped hands resting on the tabletop and saw the trace of blood beneath his fingernails. His daughter's blood. A shudder moved through him.

Last night had been a nightmare.

Children's Hospital cafeteria was nearly empty this early in the morning. A tray cart clattered out from the kitchen, bringing with it the pleasant scent of breakfast. He should eat something.

He'd been up all night, first with Alicia and then with the families of the other kids. They would all recover, thanks to Kat's fine work. Recover to face charges for breaking and entering, vandalizing. And Derek for driving under the influence. Derek even admitted writing the note on Kat's mirror in an adolescent attempt to please Alicia.

The reality that his daughter had been involved in the break-ins crushed him. Somewhere he'd failed his child.

He scrubbed at his gritty eyes.

How did a man come to grips with such a failure? Where did he go from here?

"Here you are."

He looked up. Kat offered a cup, this time of orange juice. His heart squeezed with love. She'd been here all night, as he had, holding his hand while they waited for word on Alicia, standing at his side as he went through the painful task of talking to the kids and their parents. She'd said little, but her quiet strength had kept him from falling apart. He wondered if she knew that. Even a strong man had a breaking point.

"You should go home," he said.

"Whenever you're ready."

"I'll stick around until the doctors make rounds."

"Then I'll stick with you." The chair scraped against tile as she sat down.

Yes, she'd stick with him this morning but not forever. Last night he'd seen Dr. Thatcher in action. He'd witnessed the fire in her eyes as she'd fought death and won. He'd seen the incredible skill of her gifted hands. His daughter was alive because of Kat's passion for her profession.

He'd been a selfish fool to expect Kat to give that up for him. He needed her, but the world needed her more.

He sipped the sweet juice, let the acid burn down the back of his throat.

"I don't know how to thank you for what you did," he started.

She shook her head. "Don't."

"If I'd listened to you the first time you suspected Derek, none of this would have happened."

"We don't know that. Susan would say God will work this for our good."

He almost smiled. He'd needed to hear that. "She'd be right. That's a God promise."

"Maybe this mistake saved those kids from something worse. People do learn from their mistakes, you know. Only, some of us take longer to get the message."

He frowned, trying to gauge her meaning, but his mind was too exhausted.

"What time does Rita's plane get in?" she asked.

"Ten. Did I mention how thankful I was you were here to talk to her last night?"

Alicia's mother had been on the verge of hysteria until Dr. Thatcher's cool assurance had calmed her down. Kat had even invited Rita to stay with her in Wilson's Cove until Alicia recovered enough to go home to Houston. Gotta love a woman like that.

And he did. Oh, how he did.

"Glad to be there. This is who I am, Seth. It's what I'm good at. It's where I'm needed."

He knew. Dear God, help him, he knew. He'd witnessed firsthand and was more grateful for Kat's incredible skills than he could ever say. She'd saved his child.

But somehow that didn't make losing her any easier.

Her hand closed over the top of his. "I want to tell you something." She lifted the fingers of his hand and studied them. "I made a decision about the job in Dallas."

Seth's stomach tightened. He'd had about all the heartache he could take for one twenty-four-hour period, but he'd warned himself to be ready for this. After watching her last night he'd known what she would choose, what she *had* to choose. She was leaving, heading off to Dallas and the work she loved. The love that had been growing between them all over again would be forgotten.

"You'll visit now and then, won't you?"

She tilted her head, puzzled. "No. I don't want to visit."

He swallowed. "Sure. I understand."

Make the cut clean and fast, like an incision.

"I don't think you do, Seth. I'm not taking the Dallas position. I don't want that kind of practice anymore. I want to be here in this town that needs me and loves me."

"No. You can't. You have to be a doctor. Medicine needs you."

Tears gathered in her eyes, already reddened from the long night. "Last night, as I prayed to save your daughter, I finally realized two very important things. First, I'm meant to practice medicine, but not in Dallas or any other city. That's part of why I was unhappy there. I'm meant to practice in Wilson's Cove, a place that needs me far more than Dallas ever could."

She was right about that. As hard as it was for Seth to think about, Alicia would not have survived without a doctor on the scene.

"But I thought you said . . ."

"I know what I said. I had such a negative mind-set, I'd never really considered the possibility. But I also know several physicians who are making rural practice work through creative methods. I may not get rich, but I'll be where I'm needed most and I'll be happy."

Seth began to shake inside. Like a rainbow after a storm, hope returned. "You said two things. What was the second one?"

He had a feeling he knew, but he wanted her to be the one to say it.

She paused, a flush creeping over her cheekbones. "The second thing, Seth Washington, is that I'm in love and I want to get married. To the right man. The man who's held my heart since I was sixteen years old. I know I don't deserve him. I've failed him. I've hurt him. I've made so many mistakes that I can only pray he'll forgive me. Most of all, I pray he loves me, too. Because if he doesn't, I'm making a complete fool of myself right now."

She lifted her gaze to his, eyes shining with love and unshed tears. "So what do you say to that?"

A smile started deep down and ended on Seth's lips. He was on his feet and had Kat in his arms before another second passed. He didn't care if hospital personnel were watching. All he cared was that Kat loved him enough after all.

Heart singing, he placed a kiss in her hair and said the one word one that would change his life forever.

He said yes.

EPILOGUE

Spring had returned to Wilson's Cove. Fragrance from the lilacs outside Dr. Kathryn Washington's clinic filled the air and wafted into the building each time someone passed through the door.

Kat made a notation on a patient chart and closed the folder. Running the clinic alone wasn't easy, but other than a part-time bookkeeper, Kat handled everything herself. As she'd promised Seth, she was making a rural practice work.

A smile touched her lips as she thought of Seth, her husband for eight months. Life was good. After all the years of running in a circle, stressed to the max, God had given her this slower, simpler life with the man she loved.

The pace in Wilson's Cove had returned to normal after the accident. The kids, including Derek, had gotten probation and community service for the break-ins, and from everything she'd witnessed, the near-death experience had changed them all for the better. Alicia was back in Houston, but due for her regular summer visit in a few weeks. According to her mother, she was walking the straight and narrow, truly trying to live a Christian life. During her visit over Christmas break, she'd been a different Alicia. More mature and thoughtful, she knew Kat had saved her life and now considered her stepmother a friend.

For Seth's sake, Kat was glad.

To her family's relief, the town council had successfully implemented a new leash law, incensing the owners of the pit bull so much that they'd moved away. Sadie's cat had gone on to produce another litter of kittens, one of which curled nightly at the foot of Seth and Kat's bed.

The domestic life was proving very pleasant indeed.

Hands pressed to her back, she stretched. Almost lunchtime. She could use a break. The morning had been busier than usual. Wilson's Cove residents loved the idea of a doctor in town, and her practice grew larger all the time.

Together with Seth, she'd started something else, too. She wondered how he was coming along with the project.

The door to her small main-street clinic opened. She looked up from the desk and her heart leaped. No matter how many times he walked through that door, Kat's heart filled with love and gratitude. Seth Washington had loved her when she hadn't loved herself.

"I came to take you away from all this," he said, grinning.

"My hero." Holding to the arms of the chair, she pushed to a stand.

Instantly Seth was beside her, helping as if she were fragile.

"How's our quarterback?" he said, wide hands tenderly bracketing the bulge around her middle.

"Field-goal kicker," she corrected, and they both smiled with the joy that was to come. "He's awesome."

For indeed, the ultrasound revealed a baby boy.

"So are you." He gently tugged her close and kissed her. She leaned into him for a moment, drawing in the outdoors scent of her wonderful man.

"How's the project coming?"

"The fence is finished. Want to see?" He looked as proud as she felt.

"Absolutely." Kat hung an Out To Lunch sign on the door, her cell phone number written at the bottom in case of an emergency.

Along the right front of the building, in an area that had once been a patch of grass, Seth had cultivated a small garden. Around the area, he'd erected a white border. At present, only one baby rose held its green arms toward Heaven.

Kat hoped this rose would be the only one, but she knew better. Over time, other mourning parents would need this garden of healing and it would be here for them.

"It's beautiful, honey." She slid an arm around his waist and squeezed.

The idea for a memorial garden outside the clinic had been hers, but Seth's gift of the rosebush last year had been the catalyst. When a distraught young woman had come to her, suffering a miscarriage, Kat had known what she must do. Medical care alone was not enough to heal such a loss.

"A time to heal," she said softly.

"King Solomon knew what he was talking about, didn't he?"

"Yes, he did." She turned into his arms with a smile. The gentle spring breeze played with her hair and whispered of unspeakable joy. "He also said there was a time to love."

Seth smiled down. "I pick that one."

With a thankful heart filled with contentment and joy, Kat lifted her face for his kiss.
God in His wisdom and love had known
exactly what she and Seth needed. Broken
and wounded, they'd both come home.
Home to Wilson's Cove. Home to the Lord.
Home to healing and love.

Home to each other and the baby boy stir-
ring beneath her heart.

Dear Reader,

Thank you for reading *A Time to Heal*. I hope you've enjoyed it. When I think about people like you who plunk down their hard-earned money for one of my books, I'm humbled and honored.

In this story, Kat and Seth have both made a mess of their adult lives, in part because of past issues that were never resolved. I think sometimes we humans have this tendency to carry old, worn-out baggage of the past until it dirties up our present. I know I have.

The good news, of course, is Jesus. He says we can cast our burdens on Him and move forward from past mistakes clean and new. Without that sweet promise, I'm not sure where I would be today. If you struggle with remorse or bitterness or unforgiveness, I hope you'll give it to Jesus and be healed.

313

He can handle problems so much better than we can.

If you'd like to comment on this book, I love hearing from readers. Please visit my Web site at www.lindagoodnight.com or write to me c/o Steeple Hill, 233 Broadway, Suite 1001, New York, NY 10279.

Grace and peace,
Linda Goodnight

QUESTIONS FOR DISCUSSION

1. This story took place in the tiny fictional town of Wilson's Cove, Oklahoma. How did you envision the area? What stands out in your mind about the setting? In what way did the setting add to the mood and tone of the book?

2. Who were the main characters? Did you like them and feel sympathy for them? Discuss their issues. How would you have helped each one resolve their problems?

3. Describe some of the secondary characters. Which ones seemed the most real to you? Can you identify with any of them? Why?

4. Two ladies in Wilson's Cove seemed to know everything about everybody. Seth thought their talk harmed no one. Do you agree with his assessment? What does

Scripture say about gossip? Is it gossip to pass on information about births and deaths? What exactly qualifies as gossip, in your opinion?

5. Kathryn held the remorse over her miscarriage inside for many years. Why? Discuss why suppressing emotions is a bad thing. Have you ever had a problem you felt you could not talk about? What happened? How did you deal with the feelings?

6. Kathryn had no confidence in her abilities in anything other than medicine. How did this relate to her own perceived failure to save her miscarried child? Do you think her work as a physician had anything to do with trying to "make up" for the loss?

7. Seth suffered great guilt and consternation over his divorce. Discuss the reasons for his divorce. Was there anything else he should have done to save the marriage?

8. Is divorce ever justified? Under what conditions? What are the scriptural mandates for divorce? Is remarriage ever appropriate after a divorce?

9. Kathryn had spent her life making plans that never satisfied her. Discuss some of those and why she could not find contentment. Jeremiah 29:11 talks about God's plans. Do you believe He has a plan for everyone's life? If so, what is His plan for your life?

10. Kathryn believed the miscarriage was God's punishment for the sin she committed with Seth. What do you think? Does God punish His people this way? Explain.

11. As a physician Kathryn was taught that a fetus is tissue, not a life. Do you agree? Discuss the current controversy surrounding the unborn.

12. Seth struggled with being too indulgent with his daughter. Can you understand why? Do you think there is a tendency of noncustodial parents to play "fairy godmother" when their children visit? How can this be damaging to the relationship and to the child?

13. Most children of divorce long for their parents to reunite. Do you know stepfami-

lies that have blended successfully? What do you think is the key to their success?

ABOUT THE AUTHOR

A romantic at heart, **Linda Goodnight** believes in the traditional values of family and home. Writing books enables her to share her certainty that, with faith and perseverance, love can last forever and happy endings really are possible.

A native of Oklahoma, Linda lives in the country with her husband, Gene, and Mugsy, an adorably obnoxious rat terrier. She and Gene have a blended family of six grown children. A former elementary-school teacher, she is also a licensed nurse. When time permits, Linda loves to read, watch football and rodeo and indulge in chocolate. She also enjoys taking long, calorie-burning walks in the nearby woods. Readers can write to her at linda@lindagoodnight.com, or c/o Steeple Hill Books, 233 Broadway, Suite 1001, New York, NY 10279.